The GREATEST DISCOVERY

Chris Sorensen

To Kym,

POND
PUBLISHING

Pond Publishing
9947 Hull St. #197
Richmond, VA 23236
www.pondpublishing.com

While the inspiration for this book is drawn from various personal experiences of the author, the novel is still a work of fiction. Any resemblance to actual persons is coincidental.

Publisher's Cataloging-in-Publication

Sorensen, Chris.
The greatest discovery / Chris Sorensen. -- 1st ed.

p. cm.
LCCN 2002093576
ISBN 0-9719423-1-5

1.Inspiration--Religious Aspects--Fiction.
2. Richmond (Va.) Fiction. I. Title.

PS3619.O746G74 2003   813'.6
QBI02-701341

If you would like to contact the author, you can e-mail him at:
chris@thegreatestdiscovery.com

First edition – January 2003

Printed in the United States of America

2 4 6 8 10 9 7 5 3 1

For Amanda and Michael . . .

. . . my greatest discoveries

The GREATEST DISCOVERY

1

Unsure

I swore I would never end up in the South again—at least not alive.

Even though no one considered Virginia to be in the deep South, it was far enough down that having a pick-up truck was a semi-implied requirement. I didn't even know who won the Civil War until I was in the eleventh grade, and I think that was by accident. Word must have reached the principal because the teacher mysteriously disappeared before the next school year started.

I didn't have anything against Virginia as a state, per se; it's just that I had lived there my whole life. Both my mom and dad's side of the family lived within twenty square miles of each other.

I think we arrived somewhere around the time of the Pilgrims, and none had left since—except me. My family thought I was joking when I told them I was going to college in the West.

Getting my bachelor's degree in Colorado helped me realize that the world was larger than the south side of Richmond. When I finally did finish college and moved back home to start graduate school, I didn't think people would believe that I was born and raised in Virginia. What little accent I did have before I left was lost during my four years in the Rocky Mountains.

With my bachelors behind me, I had to keep reminding myself that my master's would only take a year. At first, I was a little nervous about locking myself into a certain field; wondering if there was something else I would rather do than social work, but up to that point, everything seemed to be going okay. Sure, it had its downfalls, just like any profession, but I was pushing forward knowing that at least I wouldn't detest my job. As long as I didn't mind my work and could provide for my family, I couldn't ask for more, right?

The university in Richmond had an accelerated graduate program, which is why it would take one year instead of two. I was looking forward to only having to complete one year of coursework for my masters, but a break would have been nice. I had finished my bachelors in May, and after tying up loose ends and trucking across the country in June, my classes started the middle of July. Required courses were among the few reasons I would have voluntarily returned to the mid-Atlantic during the middle of summer.

In case you have never been to the great commonwealth of Virginia in July, it's hot. Not just "I think I need to mop my brow" hot, but "why did I bother to wear clothes out today?" hot. And driving in an old Accord with no air conditioning in the middle of lunch hour traffic didn't help, either. But my registration materials were due by the end of the week and I had to get them in because when Amanda started her job, I would be without a car.

While getting my master's degree she was the one who would be bringing in the family income. She was an art major in school that found her niche in stained glass. After applying to a few places in Richmond, her talent caught the eye of one of the local shops. The job was waiting for her when we got there. With a baby on the way, her goal was to eventually be able to do freelance work from home.

We had tried for a while to get pregnant and wasn't sure if it would ever happen, but we finally did earlier that year. She sent me some flowers at work with a little note, "We can't wait to see you when you get home," signed, "Mom and Baby." I was so excited I rushed home from work and we must have danced around the apartment for a full hour. It helped put life into perspective for both of us.

The baby was due the first week of November. We were looking forward to a remarkable Thanksgiving with plenty to be thankful for. But that was still four months away, and even though I was excited, graduate school was in the forefront of my mind.

As I pulled onto the campus, I kept wondering just how different my life was going to be. In Colorado, the college was in the middle of nowhere on a huge piece of beautifully landscaped property that sat right up against the mountains—absolute peace and quiet. All I saw in Richmond was back-to-back old buildings, cars, and fast food restaurants—very downtown. The simple task of trying to find a parking space was a stressful event. Something inside told me that life was going to be extremely different.

Luckily, my stress paid off with a spot close to the administration building. For that stint of good luck, I didn't even mind feeding the meter some change. Grabbing my paperwork, I headed for the office to voluntarily register for one more year of "higher education."

"May I help you, dear?" asked the woman behind the front desk. She was your typical white-haired, nice-as-pie southern grandmother working part time so she didn't have to sit at home.

That's one thing I could attest to without reservation: people in the South were a lot friendlier. Everyone I talked to—the secretary at the graduate office, my course advisor, and even the janitor I asked for directions—was polite and helpful.

After registration was taken care of, I wanted to check out the library to see what it had to offer. With all the time I would be spending there, I wanted to at least give it a once over, but I had to get home and begin the process of finding an internship. That was the main reason why the degree would only take one year; instead of taking the internship after completing my coursework, I would take them together.

I would take the bus to the social work building in the morning and then home from my internship at night, with studying at the library in between. I wasn't looking forward to such a hectic schedule, especially working at night, but that's what my career choice required.

My program's emphasis was rehabilitation counseling, which was the only area I really had any interest in. I worked at a drug and alcohol center in Colorado, which helped me gain a fundamental understanding of the field. There was still plenty I needed to learn, though.

As I made my way back to the car, the hustle and bustle from miles around kept ringing in my ears. I wasn't sure how quickly I could get used to being in a large city again. I was excited for the new start, but still nervous. New school, new job, different type of education—there were a lot of things to adjust to.

One of which, as mentioned, was dealing with big city parking. From thirty feet away I could see the bright green envelope neatly placed under my wiper blade. I looked at the meter and saw the red flag, then hesitantly glanced down at the ticket: *Richmond City Police, Traffic Division, July 6, $20, four minutes over.*

"Great," I said bluntly as I opened the door, frustrated. I removed my cell phone from its clip, changed the ringer from silent to normal, and tossed it onto the passenger seat. As I turned the ignition key, I noticed that the screen on the cell phone was blinking. There were four messages waiting.

After I safely got through the rush of traffic and onto the bridge I checked my voice mail. As soon as I crossed the bridge, my reception would cut out briefly while making the exchange on to the toll road.

One from my friend Bobby asking for help with his deck. Save. A hang up. Delete. Another hang up. Delete. One from Mom. She was shaken.

"Chris, this is mom. I've been trying to call you. I'm at the Women's Clinic with Amanda, the one across from Commonwealth Hospital. We came as soon as Amanda noticed she was bleeding. The number is . . . hold up . . . the number is . . ."

I frantically grabbed for a pen, but before she finished the first three digits, my reception died.

Panicked, I quickly got off at the next exit, crossed the overpass, and entered the freeway going the opposite direction. As soon as I got back on the bridge and picked up reception again I called my voice mailbox, put in my pass code, and waited for the messages to play. Before it got back to my mom's message, the phone beeped. There was another call coming in.

"Hello."

"Where are you?" my mother asked impatiently.

2

Hoping

I remember being scared.

Horrible scenes and scenarios played over in my mind. Was my wife okay? Was our baby okay?

We had gone to the doctor before we left Colorado and he said that the pregnancy was going according to schedule and the baby was healthy. We could have found out the sex of the baby, but decided against it. From our point of view, there were very few happy surprises in life, and whether we were going to have a boy or girl was one of them. Regardless of gender, we got to see the tiny hands and feet, and the small heart pumping furiously. It was like a watching a dream.

Even after seeing the baby during the ultra sound, the transformation to fatherhood was only slowly taking place. My paternal instincts were in me somewhere; they were just slowly seeping out. But after that call from my mother, my fatherly emotions came out full force. I finally understood, even if on a small scale, what it meant to be a dad. And only because for a moment, there was a thought that maybe I wouldn't be.

Thankfully, the news wasn't fatal, and my worry short lived. The experience was still eye opening, but it wasn't fatal. Amanda had been spotting, which I came to find out was not exactly serious, but something that did call for extra monitoring. The doctor said that if the bleeding stopped after a day or two and didn't come back immediately then everything would be okay.

There were still a few days before school started and I had no work responsibilities, so I waited on Amanda hand and foot. It was my way of making it up to her for not being there.

Being on bed rest for three days just about drove her crazy, but thankfully the bleeding did stop. After the doctor said everything was fine, she was back to her normal self—sort of.

She was quickly back to work and on the go again, but there was something different in the way she talked about the baby. There was a stronger bond than before, but there was also a nervousness that had appeared.

I wish she would have talked about it more, but Amanda always had a tendency to just mull things over for a while, alone, and then move on. So I didn't push the topic, and left the ball in her court. If, and when, she wanted to talk, she knew I would be there—at least periodically. School was about to start and the schedule was going to be an adjustment for both of us. The last thing either one of us needed was to be worried about the baby.

❖   ❖   ❖

How was campus? Did you get everything straight? I sure did miss you today!

I was looking forward to coming home from my first day of school and hearing any one of those statements, but Amanda wasn't home from work yet. To keep her mind occupied she seemed to find any excuse possible to not be at home alone. So either she was working late, or out seeing more of what her new hometown had to offer.

I could tell she felt more at home in Richmond than in Colorado. Being raised in suburbia Chicago, she had a lot more "on-the-run" in her than me. She was like that from the start.

We met on a blind date in Colorado. When my friend Gabe told me he was setting me up on one, I told him I wasn't *that* desperate. Then he showed me a picture and my attitude changed.

I had never seen anybody more gorgeous in my life. She was blonde, and I tended to date brunettes, but that was beside the point. Any stereotypes I had placed on blondes before were quickly erased from memory.

In no way was she typical. I had never met a more straight-headed, independent person in my life. She wasn't giggly, but she wasn't stuffy. She knew how to have fun, but wasn't into partying all the time. Nothing seemed to get her really excited or really depressed. Steady would be a good way to describe her—which was the complete opposite of me.

My brain was always twitching with activity, which would cause a spectrum of emotion from extremely excited to being down in the dumps. I wasn't spastic or anything, maybe just a little more unpredictable than the normal human being. But somehow, she fell in love with me anyway, and it's been smooth sailing since. I made her laugh and she kept me out of trouble. It worked out pretty good. We honestly had the best relationship of any couple I knew.

Unfortunately, our having a good relationship did not change the fact that I couldn't cook. Coming home and not finding her there meant that my hunger pains would have to rely solely on me. Desperate, I finally placed a frozen lasagna in the oven and sat down at the kitchen table to munch on some chips and finally look over the internship list.

There were about fifty agencies to choose from: some small, some large, some private, mostly government, all scattered around the city.

"Did you miss me?"

I leaned back in the chair to look down the hallway. Amanda was coming through the door.

"I didn't think you would ever come home."

She made her way into the kitchen, plopped down in my lap, and put her arms around my neck. "I wanted to come home to see how your first day on campus went."

I started to give her a hug, but had to retract when the smell of glass cement hit me. The stuff must have done wonders with glass, because it didn't do much for people.

She leaned in closer, and in her best French accent asked, "What, you don't like my new perfume?"

I pinched my nose and replied in a squeaky voice, "I probably would, if I was used to living on a farm."

She jumped from my lap and hit me on the shoulder. I laughed.

As she opened the oven door I heard her let out a sigh. One of the reasons I think she didn't cook more often was because she was the pickiest eater I had ever met—and it wasn't because she was pregnant. By the time she tried to decide what she actually wanted to eat, she was so hungry that the first thing edible was sufficient.

I leaned over the table to turn my attention back to the internship list.

"What are you working on?"

"I'm trying to find an internship from the list the school gave me."

"Any of them look good?" she asked as she started massaging my shoulders. I closed my eyes and let my head drop.

"You're the best wife ever," I said softly, ignoring her question.

There was no response, but I know she was smiling to herself.

"Well I'll let you get back to you work. Do you need anything?"

"I'll be fine. I promise it won't take me long." She kissed me on the top of the head, made her way to the couch, picked up a magazine, and relaxed.

Normally, I would have crossed out the agencies that did not look interesting, but I had to keep all of them in consideration in case I got desperate.

From what my advisor said, having as much previous experience as I did, I wouldn't have too much trouble finding something. Most agencies were open in the evening to accommodate client's work schedules, so I was hoping to find the directors in and set up some interviews. With my eyes closed, I spun the paper around a few times, plopped my finger down, and dialed the lucky number.

3

Possible Solitude

A twenty-five-page paper.

I tried to look on the bright side of the situation, but it was kind of hard as I pounded my forehead against the desk. The title of the book to my side, *Human Behavior in the Social Environment*, kept coming in and out of focus. It wasn't the paper that was so hard to deal with, although it was by far the largest paper I had ever been assigned to write. The fact that it was the only grade for the class made it difficult to swallow. Writing papers had never been my strong point, but I was able to keep my grades up by doing well on the other assignments. But for that class it was one chance, one grade.

The class coincided with my internship, which was to start the next day. I eventually found an agency not too far from campus, which was good news. From what I could tell, it was similar to the rehabilitation center I worked at in Colorado. My assignment was to work with the adults in the late afternoon and evening. It included group sessions as well as individual meetings.

The agency also had adolescent groups, but I had never worked with teenagers before. I always thought it would be a nice change of pace working with kids, but the chance had never presented itself. Nothing against the adults, it was just hard to relate to them sometimes; especially if they were older than me. They were almost always older than me.

As far as school went, other than the shock of the gargantuan paper I had to write, all my other classes seemed manageable. I knew they would consist of theories, studies, research, opinionated professors, and tons of rationalizing. Not that I had a hundred years of experience behind me, but from what I had gathered, the social service field was about having a caring heart and a listening ear. During the few years I did have behind me, I had met some fellow counselors who had the heart of a refrigerator.

Anyway, everything looked like it was going to be what I expected. No surprises were good surprises. But even though school and work seemed predictable, I found that the city transit system was going to hold some unique surprises of its own.

I had taken a couple practice trips, and it wasn't pretty. My choices came down to sitting next to a good-looking sorority member majoring in pre-med or early childhood education; or an old, scraggly wino at the back of the bus. Although either would offer conversation, the drunks tended to use simpler, though slurred, statements—which offered a bit of mental relief at the end of the day. I figured Amanda would agree with my seating choice, but not for the same reason.

❖   ❖   ❖

My first day of training at the agency ended early, so they let me go for the day. With a few minutes of free time, I decided to finally check out the library. As I crossed Cary Street, the big marble plaque above the front doors came into view:

The L. J. Anderson Library

All that kept running through my mind was how enormous it was—lots of glass and marble with fancy artwork and landscaping around the outside. I overheard one of the students say that it had been remodeled only five years earlier.

I walked through the rotating doors, into a huge vaulted foyer. A water fountain was positioned directly underneath a large skylight. Every five minutes blasts of water shot out from the fountain and sparkled off the sunlight.

The student worker at the information desk informed me that the social science references were on the second floor in the northeast corner. I made my way quickly up the steps, determined to stake my claim.

I was picky about where I studied. It had to be private and away from everyone, but still have a nice view so that when I got bored I'd have something to turn my attention to.

Students were spread out everywhere—some on the floor, some on the computers, while others were fast asleep. The library was different from the one in Colorado, but it was comforting to know that at least the students were the same.

An old card catalog box behind the computers caught my eye and so I walked over to it. It had been quite a long time since I'd seen one; probably not since middle school. I pulled the drawers out one by one, surprised to find that most were empty, except for a few that had Braille cards in them.

Turning my head to the right to look up at the clock, I noticed a small hallway about twenty feet long with a set of spiral stairs at the end that led upward. I looked around for a sign prohibiting me to go down the hall, but not noticing one, I headed for the stairs.

I expected to see some offices tucked out of the way, but there wasn't anything; just some random pictures hanging on the walls and the staircase.

I rearranged my backpack and looked over my shoulder. Not seeing anyone to stop me, I carefully made my way up the steps, which compared to the rest of the library, did not look, or sound, new. They groaned and creaked loudly with each step I took.

At the top of the stairs was a platform that led to an empty doorway. Three faint indentations along the frame showed where the hinges used to be. Through the doorway was a small room, maybe thirty feet wide by forty feet long. A few small, old wooden desks lined the wall on the right side of the room. The desks were spaced equally apart, each positioned directly beneath a small window.

The rest of the room consisted of chairs lining the bare left wall, and some wooden bookshelves lined up in the center. A musty smell lingered throughout.

I walked over to the right side of the room to peek out of one of the windows. The mezzanine overlooked the entrance of the library; the fountain, rotating doors, and information desk were in plain view. I turned around to get a better look.

It had all the makings of a perfect, secluded study area. The only thing that appeared out of place was that there were no books on the bookshelves; at least not the first few that I saw. But that didn't matter; there could not have been a more ideal spot anywhere in the library.

Everything seemed fine, until after a few minutes it hit me—where was everybody else? I would have thought that someplace like that, amidst thousands of other students, would have been a cherished sanctuary. They probably felt more comfortable next to the computers and leather couches, but I was more than willing to trade a little bit of comfort for peace and solitude. All I could do was hope that it was still empty the next time I came. That is, if I was allowed to be up there in the first place, which I still didn't know for sure.

Even though it was out of the way, the room appeared to be regularly visited by someone, who at least kept it dusted and organized.

"The library is closing soon."

"What?" I mumbled, turning around, my heart beating fast from the startle. Maybe I wasn't supposed to be up there after all.

An older, short, stout black man, wearing overalls, and a long-sleeved flannel shirt, was standing before me. My eyes involuntarily focused directly on his head, and the small layer of curly hairs that sat upon it. I stood there, completely still, staring. He had the whitest hair I had ever seen. It was the color of pure snow.

"The library is closing soon. It's Friday, and the library closes at seven o'clock on Fridays."

I finally took my eyes off his hair.

"Thanks," I replied, picking up my bag and heading for the door, embarrassed for staring.

"You're more than welcome to come back," he said as I passed him and made my way down the steps.

"Thanks," I said again. I was going to ask him if it was all right for me to be up there, but his invitation put my mind to rest.

On the way out, I noticed the hours on the front of the library door: Monday through Thursday 8a.m. to 11p.m., and on Friday and Saturday it closed at 7p.m. The hours made sense. Why would anyone want to hang around a library on a Friday or Saturday night?

I had called Amanda earlier to tell her to pick me up at the library, instead of at work. My cousin's birthday party was that night and it was the first time I would get to see all the family together since coming back to Richmond. I had lost track of time and we were running a little late.

Luckily, Amanda was still waiting for me outside the library. The last thing I wanted to do on a Friday night was take the bus. As I said, my options were interesting enough most nights, but add payday and a couple of extra cold ones and who knows what would have been waiting for me on the public transit system.

"Did you miss me, my dear, loving wife?" I said with all the pathetic mush I could gather. I knew it wouldn't work, it never did, but at least it would soften the moment a little.

She hadn't said anything directly, but I knew she was nervous about meeting the rest of the family. Most of them she had only met once, at our wedding reception, and some she had never met at all. In order to fit in, she was worried she might have to join a bowling league or start listening to country music.

"Are we going to get there on time?"

"Oh don't worry about it; everything's going to be fine." I could tell she was really nervous. I, on the other hand, could not have cared less what time we arrived. When we got there, we got there— everyone would be waiting for us.

"Well, maybe you should drive. That way, at least we have a chance of getting there on time."

"Either way you'll get to meet everybody. I promise it will be fine. Look on the bright side," I paused for affect, and then continued, "bowling and country music have their downfalls, but at least none of us are inbred. At least none of the family we'll see tonight . . . I think."

She did not find it amusing.

4

Not Alone

Either all of the students that studied on the second floor were blind—which would have explained the Braille catalog—or they didn't care to risk breaking any bones climbing the old staircase. At least that's what I surmised after finding the mezzanine empty again on my next visit. Empty, except for the old furniture, the bookshelves, and the books.

If there were any books on the first set of shelves the spines would have been facing me when I entered the room. But there were only books on the very last shelf in the room, which had one side pinned up against the back wall. I didn't notice the books before because I had not walked far enough

back to see them. The last shelf had only enough
books to fill it halfway.

The rest of the shelves were centered in the
middle of the room with a three-foot space in between each one that served as an aisle.

I walked to one of the desks and put my book
bag on the chair that was going to bear the imprint
of my backside for the next eleven and a half
months. I got everything situated: my laptop, text-
books, water bottle, and my favorite pen. With it
all spread out on the table in front of me in neat,
orderly piles, I sat, staring, waiting for them to put
together a masterpiece.

They stared right back.

Assignments had already begun piling up. My
orientation for work got in the way of studying the
week before, so I had to hit the books hard. Only
one week into school and I was already behind.
Luckily, my monstrous paper was not due until the
end of the semester. But that didn't stop me from
shivering every time I thought about it.

I plugged in my laptop, hoping the outlet still
had an electric current in it. Ding! The monitor
brightened up and I clicked into the word processor.
Before anything else, I wanted to type up a quick
outline of all the assignments and their due dates.
Waiting for the file to open, I pulled out my note-
books and class schedules.

As soon as my fingers hit the keys the fountain
below burst with energy and shot multiple water

sprays into the air. Whether coincidence or timing, it lifted my spirits, as if the library itself was letting me know it was rooting for me. It was a stupid thought, but mentally it helped.

I awoke to the sound of a bell faintly ringing throughout the library. It went off every hour on the forty-five minute mark to let students know it was time to head to their next class. It was loud enough to be noticed, but soft enough not to put everyone into a panic.

I had only dozed off for fifteen minutes, but it was not a good sign. I was hoping to make it at least a couple of hours before feeling drowsy.

Standing, while stretching what seemed to be every muscle in my body, I glanced around the room as the blood rushed to my head. The books on the back shelf caught my eye.

As I walked down the aisle, I ran my fingers along their spines—some with titles, some without, some old, some new, some paperback, and some hardcover. They all had call numbers on them, but they were not in any particular order, at least not like the other books in the library.

I cocked my head sideways to see if any of the titles looked familiar. The thought was doubtful, seeing as how I never took the time to read for pleasure. It's not that I didn't enjoy reading; I just never had the time.

Some of the names I recognized: Charles Dickens, Mark Twain, Emily Dickinson, Benjamin Franklin and others. Some were biographies of famous people: Washington, Lincoln, Martin Luther King, Winston Churchill, and even Bill Cosby.

"Way to go, Bill," I said, eyebrows raised, thinking of the honor that came from being placed among former respected leaders of nations. Bill probably didn't even know.

Still others, and mostly the good majority, I did not recognize: Horatio Alger, Og Mandino, Sterling W. Sills, John Steinbeck, S. E. Hinton, Napoleon Hill, Lois Lowry, and the list went on and on. There was everything from fiction, to nonfiction, short stories, long novels, poetry, business, and even a few children's books. There were some Bibles at the end of the row; or at least one Bible and other various texts, which appeared to be of a religious nature. On that small bookshelf were quite a variety of interests.

I wondered, though, why they were all sitting up there, completely cut off from the rest of the library. Except for some that looked really old, most of them seemed to be in okay condition.

"A great collection, isn't it?"

I looked through the gaps in the shelves to see the black man from the other night coming through the door. He made his way in, turned to the right, and stopped. Grabbing a handle on the wall, he gave it a turn, and then with a lift, two panels separated, one going up and the other down. It looked like an elevator of some sort.

From what I could see, there was hardly any room inside; just enough to fit the book cart it contained. There was no other way to get books up there unless they were carried up the steps, which seemed impossible. The mezzanine must have been the only part of the library that was not remodeled, as if someone high up said not to touch it.

As he pulled the book cart, which only had a few books on it, he kept talking. "It would be hard to find a better collection of books anywhere, if I do say so myself."

Again, I did not respond, but continued to watch him pull the cart while walking backwards, as if he'd done it a million times.

As he got closer, I noticed the cart had six books on it, along with a brown lunch bag.

"Do you read much?"

"Not too much," I responded. "I really don't have a lot of extra time."

He shook his head. "That's too bad." A long pause ensued as he made his way down the aisle.

"I've never seen a book cart elevator like that. Do they even still make those?" I felt I needed to say something, which would be the only reason for asking such a stupid question.

"With all the remodeling, I asked them to at least spare the stairs, the elevator, and this room."

He shook his head thoughtfully, "I couldn't bear to see them go."

Almost laughing out loud, I thought of how funny it would be seeing a volunteer, which is what I imagined he was, asking the library to do anything. I could tell he had a bit of sarcasm in him.

"Kind of like you asking them to keep all these books up here, right?"

"No," he responded, still sorting through the books, not looking at me, "that's different."

I gazed at him, puzzled, not sure what judgment call to make.

He finished his statement. "I didn't *ask* them if I could bring the books up here."

I tried to figure out why he would have wanted to bring them up there in the first place.

"These happen to be some of my favorite books. Being able to thumb through their pages any time I want is a nice luxury," he answered, as if he had read my mind.

"I've never heard of most of them."

Shocked, as if I had spoken blaspheme, he sized me up and down. Then he shrugged his shoulders and looked at me as if not surprised.

I took that a little personally, but brushed it off, not deeming it of importance. "If you're bringing all these books up here, out of the way, how would anybody expect to ever find them. Especially since you *took* them from the library?"

He laughed a little. "I did not *take* them from the library. They are still in the library, just . . . relocated."

I laughed back. "Someone would have to want them pretty bad to venture up here." Having never heard of the books myself, I couldn't see why anyone would want to make the trek up some dangerous stairs to find them.

"There's no real point in reading them unless someone really wants to. If people work for them a bit in order to find them, if they even care in the first place, the information they receive is of far more importance and much more substantial than a few rickety stairs. Besides, you found your way up here, didn't you? Maybe you'll find something up here worthwhile."

All I wanted to find was some time alone.

Part of me was trying to figure out what he was talking about, while the other part was trying to figure out why I was standing there listening to him to begin with.

Breaking the silence and changing the subject, he introduced himself, "My name is Lewis."

"Mine's Chris," I said, extending my hand.

He stepped back and retracted his hands. "It's nice to meet you, Chris, but I better not. My hands are extremely dirty," he said as he turned his palms over. I didn't see anything, but taking him at his word I smiled and lowered my hand.

"I'd better get back to what I was doing and let you get back to your studying."

I gave him a nod and left him standing in the aisle as I walked back over to my table. He did not say anything else as he finished fidgeting with the books and then rolled the cart back in front of the elevator.

Carrying his lunch bag and a book to the opposite side of the room, he sat down, took out his sandwich, and started reading. He was totally oblivious to everything else around him.

I glanced at my watch and shook my head, wondering where the time had gone. Work was expecting me soon.

I packed up my bag, grabbed my laptop case, pushed in my chair, and headed for the door. I wasn't planning to say anything to him, but I couldn't leave without asking, "How long have you worked here, Lewis?"

"Well," he said, closing his book, making sure his finger stayed in to keep his place, "I don't exactly work here."

I had already determined he was a volunteer, but I remained silent and allowed him to finish.

"I'm what you would call a . . ."

"Volunteer," I said, interrupting his sudden lapse of memory.

He rubbed his chin. "Yeah, a volunteer. You could say I have a vested interest."

I didn't have any idea what he was talking about. I really didn't care. "Okay, have a good one."

"I always do," he replied.

As I walked down the steps, I couldn't help but think that he seemed a little odd. He didn't seem mental or anything, there was just something about him—something different.

5

Slow Start and a *New Friend*

After only three weeks into school I could tell I should have taken a summer vacation. The classes weren't hard; they just got boring. Not that I had never been in boring classes before, I had been in plenty, but I expected my graduate work to be a little more centralized, a little more interesting.

But most of the time we would end up sitting around in groups discussing certain concepts and ideas in very detailed conversations. I didn't have anything against any of the students in the class; I just expected a more hands on approach to learning. Maybe some more out in the field type of activities.

Anyway, I still had a little over four months to go, and that only got me to Christmas break. If I was ever going to make it, my frame of mind had to stay focused.

At least work at the agency was going well and I was beginning to establish relationships with my clients. One of the directors would lead the group meetings while I helped encourage discussion among the clients. Group sessions were okay, but I enjoyed the one-on-one time I had with clients during personal sessions more.

Sometimes I made a difference, sometimes I didn't. It seemed everybody who walked through the agency doors had been through many programs already. From my experience, the majority would use drugs or alcohol again, but there were those who had come to their last straw and were ready to make a change. They were sick of being addicted. The other clients were stopovers who would gain some experience and then move on, allowing another program to be the one to click with them. My goal was to try and help bring about a change sooner rather than later.

❖   ❖   ❖

It did not take me long to figure out that the best part of the week would be spending time with Amanda on Friday nights, and sleeping in on Saturday.

She was flipping through the TV channels as I walked over and kissed her on the cheek.

"How was work?" I asked, and walked into the kitchen to look in the fridge. My stomach had been growling for two straight hours.

"It was good," she responded, more out of habit than actual truth, I think—although she rarely had bad things to say about work.

"One of the girls at work had a sister who lost her baby today." I stood with the fridge door open, listening. There was a long pause.

I closed the door, slowly, and walked to the opening in the living room. I tried, but couldn't think of anything insightful to say.

"I'm sorry to hear that," I responded, leaning against the wall, giving her my attention. Her eyes were filled with worry, depression, and a whole range of other emotions.

When we first realized it was going to be difficult to get pregnant, a lot of feelings were involved. Then when we did get pregnant, well, I can't explain the gratitude we felt.

But deep down, Amanda always had some sense that things were going to be rough in order to have the baby. It was a stronger feeling when we first found out we were pregnant, but she slowly started to become more positive, and then the scare with the spotting . . . it just brought all those feelings of uncertainty back again.

After that, every time she heard less than positive news about a pregnancy it got her mind rolling
again. Almost like she was dreading all the horrible scenarios she might have to go through.

I moved closer to sit next to her on the couch.
Before I got to her, she stood up, grabbed my hand,
and walked down the hall into the bedroom.

She got into bed, and I followed, with my
clothes, shoes, and everything still on. I wanted
her to know it was going to be okay. I felt like it
would be, but I wanted her to feel that way, too. I
put my arm around her and held her close as she
cried us both to sleep.

❖   ❖   ❖

I awoke to the sound of loud, squeaky footsteps
coming from the stairs. As I turned my head from
side to side to stretch, I knew it was Lewis. It was
Tuesday and lunchtime, and he was like clockwork.

When I opened my lunch bag I found that
Amanda had taken the time to pack it for me. I
should have gotten her to pack it everyday. It was
the same food I would have chosen, but somehow it
looked a little more edible coming from her.

"Well, how goes it, Mr. Chris?" Lewis asked
cheerfully as he walked through the door, as happy
and content with life as he was every day.

I couldn't help but smile. "Doing good, Lewis.
I'm hanging in there."

"It looks like you're sitting in there," he replied, grinning, and then he winked at me and walked over to the elevator. I shook my head. His statement reminded me of my grandfather—corny, but he knew it and did it on purpose.

Lewis worked, or volunteered, a regular schedule: Tuesdays, Thursdays, and Saturdays for four-hour shifts, and Friday night closing. Except for Friday, all of his other shifts coincided with lunch. I saw him every week, at least on Tuesdays and Thursdays. Mostly we went about our business; I to my schoolwork, and he to his books and lunch.

He seemed simple enough; he had a good heart and enjoyed his work. I kind of envied him in a way. I couldn't remember ever meeting anyone who was always so happy and at peace with things. He didn't seem to worry about anything.

I still didn't know that much about him, though. We exchanged short sentences every now and then, but we never sat down and had a real conversation, even though he seemed like someone who could talk if given the chance. I think he hesitated for fear of taking me from my studies, which I appreciated.

"What? Not studying hard today?"

"Just taking a break," I said, rubbing my eyes. As an undergraduate, I learned not to get tense if everything that needed to get done did not get done. A little break every once in a while never hurt anybody.

He stopped before he made it back to his books and looked at me. "Are you getting ready to eat lunch?"

"Yeah, I am. I think I'm going to put off my studying for today and take it easy."

"Well, I don't want to condone you in not studying, but everybody does need a break now and then." I nodded in agreement as he pulled out his lunch bag.

"I'm kind of feeling hungry a little early today. Mind if I eat with you?" he said, patting his stomach with his palm.

I didn't buy it; he saw the opportunity for conversation and jumped at it. But I didn't mind—I was happy to have the company. "Please do."

As he walked over I realized the whole month I had been in Richmond I hadn't really made any friends. There were the students in my classes and my co-workers that I was getting to know, but no special bond beyond acquaintances. It was kind of depressing. I missed having good, old-fashioned guy conversation. Well, Lewis was not just another guy—not that he wasn't a . . . you know what I mean. I imagined that when I got back to Virginia, any guy friends I did meet would be a little more my age.

To his credit, though, for as old as he looked, he sure did have good mobility. He had to be at least in his late sixties or early seventies. Not that I was used to hanging out with older people, but he seemed above average in physical attributes. I remember thinking that if when I got to be his age I could move around half as well as he did, I would be grateful. Hopefully by then I would still have all my teeth, too, but I wasn't about to ask him about that. There were other things I wanted to find out about him first.

The teeth could wait.

6

64 Squares

All of the stuff I said about how things seemed like they were going to be manageable and predictable; well, it wasn't true—only wishful thinking.

Maybe things were a little different than I thought they would be. Work still wasn't horrible, but having more authority than I was used to opened my eyes to some negative aspects of the career I had chosen. As the weeks went by I realized more and more that there were so many different opinions about what would or wouldn't make a difference in the lives of the clients. It seemed like everybody was going in circles—the clients as well as the agency advisors.

And to make matters worse, I had also been brought out of my idealistic notion that decisions were made based on what was best for the client. As it turned out, most of the decisions were based on money, of which there never seemed to be enough. I understood that money was needed to run the agency, it couldn't survive without it, but since we were dealing with people's lives, decisions shouldn't have always been determined by how much was in the bank.

With my understanding of the realistic mechanics of my profession slowly increasing, I also acquired a bad taste in my mouth for my classes.

The professors would get me all excited about making a difference and helping people and being "equipped" with the tools I needed, and then BAM—oh, you can't do that because there's not enough money or that's discriminating or somebody could sue us. All the theories and patterns could make a difference, but only if someone was able to get through all the red tape.

By the time I got to the library, my brain hurt. It was nice out, so I sat on one of benches outside, directly underneath a dogwood, and drew in a deep breath. Taking my glasses off, I slowly massaged my eyes, and exhaled.

Maybe it was good for me to have my eyes opened early; instead of after I graduated and got a full-time position. If I had to put up with similar circumstances everyday for a full eight hours, I wouldn't have been able to handle it. The thought of looking into private agencies crossed my mind. Because their budget wasn't passed through government channels, they usually had fewer hoops to jump through, more money, and more say with their programs.

Leaning forward on the bench, I put my chin in my hands and slowly breathed in and then out again. All I wanted to do was find a job. I did not want to let the little things get to me.

When I finally walked through the opening of the mezzanine, all I could think about was sitting back, eating my lunch in peace, and relaxing a little.

But I knew that was going to be impossible when I saw Lewis already seated at the table. Don't get me wrong; we had a good lunch the other day, just chitchatting about this and that—the weather, my family, and baseball. It was a nice break to sit and talk with him. I just couldn't afford to do it everyday.

"Do you like to play chess?" he asked enthusiastically, before I even had a chance to put my things down.

"I do," I answered, sitting down to pull out my lunch bag. "I really don't play that much, though; every now and then with my dad." I did enjoy playing, but I was not very good. Chess gave me a chance to spend time with my dad, even though he always beat me.

With a childish joy, one in which he tried in vain to hide, Lewis made his way over to the elevator shaft and opened the door. He knelt down and found a small storage unit at the back of the elevator. He pulled the panel loose, reached in, and brought out an object. As he started back towards me, the box came into focus—it was a chess set.

He held it in his hands like a valued heirloom. As he brushed off the top, a stream of dust went spiraling through the air. It must have been sitting in there for quite awhile.

After the dust settled, Lewis still had a huge grin on his face as he laid it on the table. It appeared to be a very nice set, older, with a shiny finish over the wood. Two copper clasps on one side held it together, and when unfastened, the set unfolded to reveal the pieces neatly arranged on the inside. They each were lying against a row of green felt, held in place by little hooks that fit every piece with precise snugness. Without saying a word, he began unfastening the pieces and placed them on the table.

After the last pawn was out, Lewis flipped the chess set over. As I bit into my sandwich, he wiped what dust remained off the top with his handkerchief. It really was a good-looking set, and the chess pieces almost looked . . .

"My father hand carved the pieces," Lewis said respectfully as he broke the silence and stole my thought. Lewis's father must have been a man with a lot of time on his hands. The pieces were amazingly similar—size, shape, and color.

"Well, are we going to play or what?" he asked, his solid, experienced hands placing the darker chess pieces on the board, facing me.

After the pieces were arranged, I moved my knight into play, and the real conversation began. We exchanged phrases equally the last time we were together, but that day, because I was frustrated, I controlled the conversation.

There was something about being able to have a nice, uninhibited talk while my mind was concentrating on the chessboard. I could be open and honest, conveying my true feelings with no restraint. Thoughts and phrases snuck out that may not have been uttered during a moment of rational consciousness.

I laid out all my worries over the recent discoveries with work and school. With his age and whatever experience he had, I was sure Lewis would be able to relate and share his own tales of school or career frustration. No response came from him, though; only an occasional nod to let me know he was paying attention. So I just kept talking.

After thirty minutes I was one move away from being put into check and fresh out of things to say, though I felt better. Being able to vent a little helped to put my mind at ease, I guess.

With nothing else to say, I stared at Lewis, waiting to see if he had anything to add.

"Well," he said slowly, still studying the board. He paused for a moment as he continued to focus his attention on the chess pieces. I sat there and waited for him to finish his response.

"Well, if I looked at things like you do I would probably feel the same way. It would be tough," he said with a confirming nod of the head, and then went back to studying the board. He didn't say anything else.

Squinting, I looked at him and wondered why he had said that. It was the way he said it, almost derogatorily. What was that supposed to mean anyway, 'If I look at things like you do'? The longer I sat thinking about it, the more disturbed I became by his statement. He placed his hand on his bishop.

"Are you saying I'm looking at things wrong?" I asked defensively, but calmly.

Still not looking at me, Lewis answered, his fingers on the bishop. "The way I see it, you are just looking at things from your perspective, trying to get it all figured out. We all have bad days and have to find some way to try and make sense of all that's going on."

I nodded in agreement. I had been through a rough day and was trying to figure out how to deal with it. That was the natural thing to do. Being able to talk out my troubles with someone else was what I needed. At the time, Lewis just happened to be the most available person for the job.

But it didn't matter anymore. I was done talking.

We finished the game in silence. I let Lewis have the run of the board, while I tried little moves here and there to see how he would respond. I was moving my pieces, but not really paying attention to them. For the remainder of the game, I sat thinking about what Lewis had said, and I slowly decided not to let it get to me. His statement wasn't mean or hurtful; maybe it just came out wrong, or he didn't know what else to say. I don't know why I got so defensive with him; Lewis didn't seem like the type to try and offend someone for the fun of it.

After he put me into checkmate, I rested my hands behind my head, thankful it was over. He started to put away the chess pieces and I thanked him for the game, and taking the time to listen to me babble. I was going to apologize for taking offense, but since he didn't bring it up, I decided to let it go.

"I don't want to take you from your studies that much, but would you like to play again sometime?"

As I left the mezzanine, feeling at least a little better about my circumstances, I replied, "Sure."

❖   ❖   ❖

Chess became a weekly activity. Actually, it was more like a biweekly activity. I thought once a week was going to be pushing it for me, but breaks kept getting easier and easier to take. Every Tuesday and Thursday, after I did get a little studying in, we would take our places around the table, get out our lunches, and set up the board.

Sometimes the games went on too long and we were not able to finish because I had to head to work. When that happened, Lewis drew out the placement of the remaining pieces on a piece of paper so we could resume play the next time we got together. It was tedious, but it was the only way we could remember where we left off, because at the end of every game the chessboard found its way back into the storage space in the elevator—Lewis made sure of that.

I became accustomed to the time we spent together and looked forward to it each week. Between work, school, and everything else, an hour or two a couple of days a week offered the little breaks I needed.

Amanda was just happy that I had found someone to, as she put it, "pal around with." I kept telling her that she needed to come up one day; Lewis would love to meet her. We just had never taken the time to arrange schedules in order for it to happen.

Most days we played chess, ate lunch, and talked about whatever. I still didn't know that much about him, though. He kept any personal info pretty tucked away.

I knew what he was like from being around him; he rotated between bologna and turkey sandwiches every other day, he couldn't stand carbonation, and he hated foreign cars. But I didn't know anything about his personal history; where he grew up, what he did for a living before the library, or if he had any kids. The subject of marriage did come up once, but he said that his wife had left him years before, so it was a topic I tried to avoid.

Most days, as I said, we had nice, friendly conversations, but sometimes I felt like venting. And when I felt like it, I did; and Lewis would sit back and let me. He was very patient that way. He wasn't my psychiatrist or anything—though he probably felt like it sometimes. There was one day in particular I remember, though, that really got the ball rolling.

"You wouldn't believe it, Lewis," I said, finally standing to give my body more room to move. "Once a week we have a recreational therapist come in and we take the group members out on an activity. Most of the time it's an activity to help them learn teamwork and trust, like a ropes course or something similar. But yesterday the advisory board *advised* us that there is not enough money in the budget to continue the activities. I wanted to go off on somebody.

"Sure, there isn't money for *everything* that is needed at the agency, but these activities are one of the best rehabilitators for clients. It's pretty amazing to see them put their trust in other people, relying on each other, and using teamwork. Especially since most of them have never put their trust in anything other than drugs or alcohol.

"It's starting to really get hard; trying to figure out how to deal with all the politics involved. You can't do this, you can't say that, it offends people or they're not ready for it, or do it this way, or be careful about this, we don't have the finances for that, blah, blah, blah, blah, blah, blah."

Lewis broke his silence and started laughing. My hand gestures during "blah, blah, blah" probably were a little animated. But I was on a role, so I kept going.

"And then this morning, what is the first thing we talk about in my intervention class: the positive side effects of recreational therapy. There are too many rules and stipulations. The system would be better if they allowed you to skip school and just start working, because the things you learn in school, they don't allow you to use in real, everyday settings anyway. There are too many 'what-if's' involved. It's all too suggestive."

When Lewis moved his queen, I put my brain on pause for a few seconds, moved my bishop, and started again. "One of my friends from high school went into accounting, and his job keeps it simple:

you make this, you spend this, you pay this, divide this by that, and voila, it's done."

"So are you saying you would rather be an accountant?" Lewis interrupted sarcastically.

"Of course not, I would hate it. Sitting behind a desk working with numbers . . . uh-uh, not me."

Lewis continued to study the board as I sat down to cool off and tried to rationalize myself back to some form of positivism.

"At least doing social work, I won't end up working for the rest of my life doing something I *really* hate. I just wish it wasn't so complicated."

"Chris," Lewis said thoughtfully, pondering his move. He retracted his hand from his knight and, forgetting the board altogether, looked at me.

Staring, he did not say anything. I could tell he wanted to say something, but he just sat there and looked at me. Finally, he turned his attention away from me, and went back to the board.

"Okay Lewis, you have my attention."

He straightened himself in his chair and proceeded, as if he already knew what he wanted to say and had just been waiting for the right opportunity. "Do you think it would be all right if I make an observation?"

"Sure," I replied, thankful I wasn't going to have to pry it out of him.

He focused his gaze on me for what seemed like forever, then leaned forward and asked, "Are you happy, Chris?"

Taken by surprise, I didn't respond. How could he ask me if I was happy? It seemed like such a vague question.

While fidgeting around in my chair, I indirectly answered, "I think the main reason I complain is that it gets overwhelming sometimes, having to do school and work. It seems like that's all I do. Once school is over and I get out in an agency full-time, I'll have a little more time on my hands. I mean, I like helping people, and this has been a good field for me. Everybody has little quirks in their job. Nobody has the perfect job.

"You find the best you can, try to do some good, and try to focus on the positives more than the negatives. That's why the times I get to share things with you, at least the negative things, it helps me deal with the situation and put life back into perspective. I am getting a great education and will be able to provide for my family and help some people in the process. Who can ask for more?"

When he didn't respond, I became more uncomfortable, so I continued. "I hope you don't feel like that's *all* I do is complain to you. I really appreciate you letting me blow off steam every now and then. If I was to complain to Amanda, she would only get worried, and there's really nothing to worry about."

Lewis leaned back in his chair and calmly pointed out, "You didn't answer my question."

I sat there, dumbfounded, not sure what else to say. If he didn't want to accept my answer, that was his problem. After ten seconds of silence, we both realized I wasn't going to say anything else.

"Tell you what," he said, standing up and placing his empty lunch bag in his pocket. "Why don't you think about it for a few days, and then we will get back together on Tuesday. Regardless of what your answer is, I have something I want to share with you. You don't have to agree with me, all I ask is that you listen."

I nodded, involuntarily.

After nodding back, he left me there, alone, to put away the chess set—and to think about something that I had never really taken the time to think about before.

7

Searching for Answers

Well sure I was happy! That's what I told myself that whole weekend. Life was good and I was
happy. I just wasn't able to say it when Lewis
asked—and that bugged me.

Whatever it was that Lewis wanted to share
with me, I was at least going to listen. My curiosity
was piqued too much to do otherwise. I didn't know
what it was that made me pause, but I promised
myself I wouldn't let it happen again.

When I reached the mezzanine and found no
sign of Lewis, I began studying. I had a ton of assignments due the following week. From my experience, the middle of the semester was always the

busiest. I think the professors had some sort of evil conspiracy.

When Lewis finally wandered in, I closed my book to give him my full attention. He didn't appear to be his usual upbeat self. Not that he looked upset; he just looked a little more concentrated, a little more focused than normal.

"Hi, Lewis. How was your weekend?"

"Good."

He did not even make his way over to the elevator to fetch his cart; instead, he came over and sat down at the table. I could tell he was serious. He had not forgotten our conversation from Thursday.

"I took you up on your suggestion, and have been thinking about what you asked," I stated, wanting him to know that I had not forgotten either.

He brushed off my statement, almost ignoring it, sat down, and began.

"Chris, what I have to say may be a more in depth answer than you expected. You don't have to agree with me. All I ask is that you at least listen. Does that sound fair enough?"

"I've already decided that I will at least hear what you have to say."

He did not waste anytime. "There are three things I've learned over the years that have helped me put life into perspective. Now there are a lot of different things that we all learn along the way, but these are my base, my foundation that have helped me make it through with a smile on my face and peace in my heart. I am sharing them with you because after two months of listening to all that you're going through, I feel it might be of benefit."

My eyebrows rose at Lewis's bluntness. I remained silent.

"Do you believe that people are unique?"

I thought to myself for a second. "Well, yeah, that's pretty much common knowledge. Everybody's different in their own way."

I hoped that wasn't his first lesson. I needed something a little more substantial than "everyone's unique."

"What makes each of us unique?"

I shrugged. "I don't know; lots of things." A few hundred of them ran through my mind, but I couldn't pinpoint one in particular to mention.

Lewis shook his head. "Typical," he said softly under his breath, followed by a huff of air from his nose. He reached into his lunch bag, pulled out an apple, and placed it on the table.

"I want you to find out how many seeds are in this apple." He paused to make sure I was listening. "Then, I will meet you here again on Thursday."

He wished me good luck and not saying another word, he left me alone—again.

Sitting, staring at the apple, I couldn't help but wonder what I had gotten myself into. Was Lewis ever going to give me a straight answer?

❖   ❖   ❖

Somewhere inside I tried to rationalize and draw some type of sanity out of what Lewis asked me to do. Find out how many seeds were in an apple?

It was crazy.

But what was even crazier is that I did it. It was messy, but I did it. The people at work probably thought I had finally lost it; sitting in the lunchroom tearing a helpless apple to shreds.

But after careful effort and meticulous rummaging through sticky pulp, I had eight lifeless seeds lying in front of me. What was the point? Why should I have cared how many seeds were in the apple?

Rolling my eyes and shaking my head, I placed the seeds in a sandwich bag. After I finished my shift at work, I headed home for the day, frustrated.

When I entered the apartment, I found Amanda sprawled out on the couch fast asleep. Normally, I wouldn't have dared wake her, but it was almost bedtime. After sitting down on the arm of the couch, I started massaging her foot. She must not have been completely asleep, because she immediately turned on her back and extended her other foot.

After what had to be the longest foot rub in history, she finally gave me permission to stop. I moved closer to her and placed my ear on her stomach to see if I could hear anything.

"What do you think it is?" she asked as she slowly started to rub my hair.

"I don't know, a seed," I said sarcastically, still flustered that Lewis had not just come out and told me what he wanted to tell me. Why did I have to go through so many hoops?

"Huh?"

"Never mind. I was just being stupid."

"Are you doing okay? How are things going with school?"

"Oh, everything's fine. School and work are the same old, same old. Lewis is just giving me the runaround about something."

"What do you mean?"

"It's nothing. I'll tell you about it later. I'm just tired and a little cranky." Not wanting to probe, she continued running her fingers through my hair. I turned my attention back to her original question and answered, "Anyway, I'm no psychic, but I would say that we have a fifty-fifty chance of either having a boy or a girl."

"That's cute," she said as she gave my hair a pull.

"Ouch," I yelled while sitting up to take the defensive. She just smiled. Not having to worry about another attack, I leaned back comfortably into the couch.

"Either way, speculating doesn't make much of a difference now." I put my hand on her stomach. "We'll find out soon enough."

8

First Lesson

As usual, I found myself waiting for Lewis in the mezzanine. That small room had begun to grow on me; it was like a second home. The numbers that ran through my head brought a depressing thought—I actually spent more waking hours at the library than I did at home.

"Do you ever sleep at home?" Lewis asked loudly as he made his way over to the elevator cart. Almost without fail I seemed to fall asleep on Thursdays while studying. End of the week wind down I guess. Lewis loved to tease me. "Do you get extra credit for all that sleep?"

"Ha-ha," I replied. "That's real funny."

He snickered to himself. I expected him to have on his serious face again, but he proved me wrong. Quickly getting back into routine, he grabbed his cart and headed for the back aisle.

Had he forgotten about the apple?

I knew he hadn't. He was trying to get to me. Somehow he didn't think I was serious about listening to what he had to say. That was why he huffed under his breath the other day and called me "typical." He needed to know he was wrong.

"Well, I found out how many seeds were in the apple."

"Uh-huh," he replied, uninterested.

I told him that the apple had eight seeds in it and then I waited for a response. He just nodded.

"So what does that have to do with the first lesson?" When no response came, I asked again, louder.

I watched him through the shelves as he walked to the end of the row. Leaning against the end of the shelf, his arms folded, he started. "Well . . ." he paused for a second, rubbing his chin, "it has quite a lot to do with it," and with a nod he walked back down the aisle.

My hands flew into the air. I couldn't take anymore. "All right, Lewis!" I said demandingly and waited for him to show himself again. "Enough with the books! Come here, sit down, and share with me the wisdom of the apple seeds."

To Lewis, it probably sounded a little sarcastic, but he got my point, and made his way to the table.

"So, you like all these questions, huh?" he asked, half laughingly, as he sat down.

"No," I replied bluntly. "I'm all ears, just talk and tell me what I was supposed to learn from these apple seeds, and it better be good!"

He raised his hands in defeat. "Okay, okay, I'll talk."

After I calmed myself down I signaled for him to begin.

"So the apple had eight seeds in it?" he asked. Hesitating, I almost didn't answer. I had told him no more questions; he wasn't going to get me to do all the talking.

"Yes, it had eight seeds."

"Do you still have any of the seeds with you?"

I reached into my backpack, pulled out the plastic bag, and handed it to Lewis. He took one of the seeds out and held it carefully between his fingers. "So it's possible to find out how many seeds are in an apple, right?"

"Yes. It's a little tricky, but yes."

He motioned for me to put my hand out, which I did, and then he placed the seed in my palm.

"When I asked you whether you believe that each of us, as people, are unique, you said that you agreed. Over the years I have also come to believe that each of us are unique. Each of us has special talents and abilities—you could call them gifts—

that we have been given." He then looked back down at the seed in my hand and pointing to it, said, "Each of us has these gifts, just like every apple has its seeds. In a way, they are like the seeds that are in each of us."

My eyes involuntarily rolled with the anticipation of some cheesy analogy that sounded good, but had no practical meaning. Images of late night self-help commercials came to mind.

"Is there something wrong?" he asked, sensing my apprehension.

"No, no," I said, trying to regain my composure, "I'm just trying to keep up and take it all in." I tried to give him my complete attention; I promised him I would at least do that much before making any judgment calls.

"So you're saying that the seeds are an analogy to illustrate how each person has special abilities that help make them who they are; just like each seed has the ability to become an apple. Am I close?" I asked

"So far so good," he said, smiling. "Do you agree with that analogy?"

I rocked my head back and forth and pondered the question. I didn't think twice about blurting out that everyone was unique. That was a piece of information that the whole world knew: different physical traits, attributes, temperaments, sense of humor and so on. But what about a person's abilities and talents and so-called gifts? I couldn't help but agree with him. It just made sense.

"Sure, I can buy that."

Lewis nodded and then leaned back in his chair. "If you agree with that, Chris, then what are *your* seeds?"

I put my elbows on my knees and sat, staring at the floor. Maybe I had bought into what he said too quickly.

Out of desperation, I said the first thing that popped into my head.

"As far as special or unique abilities go, I think I get along with people pretty good. I mean, I don't really have any enemies. I'm not sure if that qualifies as what you call a seed or any special gift, though," I replied, not knowing if I was on the right track. My supervisor at the agency had recently told me that she was glad to see me getting along with everyone. That's probably why it had come to mind.

"That's a fine example. You feel you have a special ability to get along with people. You seem to like everyone and everyone seems to like you. Nobody is really holding any grudges. Is that how you feel?"

"Pretty much, I guess."

"Not everyone can say that, Chris. Some people are easily offended, or they are the type that easily offends others."

I nodded in agreement and impatiently asked, "So is that the first lesson—that everybody has special talents and abilities?"

"Well, that's the start of it. I think if anyone actually stopped to think about it, as you have today, they would agree that everyone is unique. The biggest problem, I think, is that most people don't ever take the time to stop and think about it.

"I would say you're even a little above average because you were actually able to think of a special seed you have. If most people were asked, I would wager that they wouldn't have any idea."

When he paused to clear his throat, I interrupted.

"Forgive me for being blunt, Lewis, but does it really make a difference? I mean, if the majority of people are generally happy, does it really matter if they take time to stop and think about why? In a way, aren't they living according to their talents and abilities, maybe just without knowing it? What's wrong with that?"

"At first glance there is nothing wrong with it," he answered. "If someone leads a happy life and they are pleased with their circumstances, then they probably are using their seeds, even if they don't know it. But . . ."

He thought about his statement, and continued. "The first lesson is that we do have unique talents and abilities, or gifts; but more importantly, we need to come to a realization of what those gifts are; of what seeds we have inside us."

I rose from my chair, slowly, and walked over to lean on one of the bookshelves. It took him a whole week to tell me that. I felt short changed.

"But I still don't understand what difference it makes whether we know or not."

Lewis quickly glanced down at his watch, and with a 'where did the time go' expression, brought the discussion to a close. "That is the first thing I wanted to share. I will save the answer to your question until Tuesday. If you think about it over the weekend, you may be surprised at some of the different answers you may come up with.

"Regardless of what you come up with, though, I'll at least give you my answer to the question. It should lead right into the second thing I'd like to share."

I wanted to be frustrated. I just wanted him to give me the stupid answer, but I didn't say anything. In a way I was interested to see what answers I could come up with. It almost felt like a challenge, like I needed to fit the pieces of a puzzle together.

Besides, I had no reason to be mad at Lewis. He never promised me anything, except that he would share his three thoughts with me. And even then, he never said he would share them all at once.

"Thanks, Lewis," I said as I packed my stuff up to get ready to leave. It wasn't worth pursuing anymore; I had to get to work anyway. But a question came to mind as I started for the door, and I couldn't leave without asking it. "Just out of curiosity Lewis, why do you call them gifts?"

He put his chin in his palm, and resting his elbow on the arm of the chair, answered, "Because they have been given to us."

Given to us by wh–, I thought to myself, almost asking him out loud. But I stopped, not wanting to finish the question. Something inside told me what his answer would be, and the discussion was deep enough already without bringing up religion.

I nodded, making my face appear as if I was pondering what he said. Then, after thanking him again, I left him sitting at the table all by himself. He was not going to leave me alone a third time—I had decided that before the conversation began.

9

Second Lesson

"Well, I came prepared for the second lesson," I said as I reached into my lunch bag and pulled out a knife. The apples taught me a lesson, so I made sure I was ready for anything. Lewis laughed a little and made his way over to the table.

He seemed a little more relaxed. I think he finally realized that I was serious about listening to him. At least I hoped he did, anyway.

I hadn't been able to stop thinking about what he asked me; or I guess, what I asked him. Why?

Why did we need to realize what our talents and abilities were? What did it matter? I had been racking my brains all weekend.

After some serious mental debates, I thought I had come up with an answer. I still wasn't sure if I came up with it because I actually believed it, or because I just wanted to have something to say to Lewis. At the time, I didn't care.

"I've had plenty of time this weekend to think about 'why' Lewis and I've come up with an answer. At least an answer that helps me understand, even if a little, why we might need to think about and find out what our talents are."

Lewis relaxed in his chair, and gave me his attention.

"The reason we need to realize what our personal seeds are is because of all that needs to get done in the world. I mean, it's almost as if everyone has to be different in order to accommodate all that takes place in the world—different occupations, lifestyles, goods, services, family responsibilities, and so on."

"But that still doesn't answer the 'why'," Lewis pointed out, rushing me. I was just about to finish my comment before he cut me off.

After making sure he wouldn't interrupt me again, I continued. "*And,* the reason why we need to know what our talents are is to give us a better chance of heading in the right direction."

Lewis nodded and asked, "I can see what you're getting at, but what do you mean by 'the right direction?'"

"Well, there are all the different roles that need to be filled and the many directions a person can take. You have teachers, policemen, legislators, bankers, nurses, and this, that, and the other. If everyone were the same we'd have to force people to fill a particular need. But with everybody having different abilities and desires, everyone gets a chance to personally fill a specific role. Having a choice, people have a better chance of being happy."

I paused and gave him a chance to reply.

"So because of our individual uniqueness, along with all the roles that need to be filled, are you saying that most people are satisfied with their career choice, or whatever it is that they do for a living?"

"I guess that's what I am saying," I said, vaguely concluding my statement.

His eyes wandered off into space as he thought for a moment, and then looked back at me again.

"That's something we mentioned the other day. You asked why would a person need to know specifically what talents they have if they are already happy with their life."

Remembering the statement, I nodded.

"Then how many people do you know Chris who are happy with their life? How many people do you know who really enjoy what they do for a living—be it a homemaker, CEO or whatever? And don't count people who are just content or complacent with their work; I mean people who actually love what they do and look forward to it everyday."

Without effort, names flooded my mind. There were plenty of people who I considered content, and because of that they were happy, but apparently that wasn't going to work for Lewis. So I tried to concentrate and think of people I knew who would fit his parameters.

The seconds went ticking by; my brain turned, but no names came. After a while, I didn't want to say anything, because, to be honest, I couldn't think of a single person.

My dad was a definite no. Mom didn't necessarily hate her job, but if they offered her early retirement she wouldn't complain. The people at work, my extended family, and friends also fell into the content category.

All of a sudden I blurted out, "Amanda! She enjoys working with stained glass. She has her bad days, just like anyone, but they are very rare." I let out a sigh, thankful I had thought of someone. "I would definitely say she loves what she does."

"Why do you think that is?" Lewis asked.

"It's what she's always wanted to do. Well, maybe not always. She was an art major in school and did not seem to be enjoying it very much. She considered herself an artist and wanted to do something in the field, but nothing seemed to be clicking with her. Then she took a stained glass class and that was it, she was hooked. It was like everything she had been looking for to express herself just fell into her lap and after the class was finished, she knew that's the direction she wanted to follow.

"She found out there were two stained glass studios in the area, and she gave them a call. One of them asked her to come in and show them some of her work. They had an opening, liked her work, and told her she could start the very next week. Being in school, she was torn between finishing school or taking the job. But she knew a bachelor's degree in art would not have done much for her professionally, so she took the job. Even though everyone thought she was crazy for dropping out, I couldn't help but be behind her one hundred percent. She just seemed so happy."

"Using her as an example, then, what is her purpose for doing stained glass?"

I briefly thought about his question, and then said, "Probably because she really feels like she is contributing something. Like she has a special . . ." I stopped. The word I was about to say came flashing across my eyeballs in big, bold letters—GIFT.

Lewis just sat there, grinning.

I finished my statement. "I guess she feels like she is making a difference, like she has something to give. That's why she enjoys it, because it's not really work to her."

Lewis accepted my explanation and began to probe me some more. "Who are some others you can think of who really enjoy what they do?"

I thought, again, but still I drew a blank. I finally confessed, "Honestly, Lewis, I really can't think of anyone. I can't even mention myself. Most of the people fall into the 'being content' category, but you probably already knew that."

Lewis smiled again, and another name hit me.

"Well, now that I think about it, I could add you to the list. You seem to take satisfaction out of what you do."

"You're right, I do," he answered affirmatively. "So have you ever thought about that before? Out of all the people you know, you can only come up with two, on a moment's notice, who really enjoy what they do for a living. Why do you think that is?"

"I think mostly it's because they would rather be doing something that fits more with them, more with their personality. Going along with what you've been talking about, something that fits with their talents and abilities. The only problem is they don't really know what it is they would rather be doing."

The words hit me as they came out of my mouth. Lewis grinned as I inadvertently proved his point from the first lesson.

I reluctantly admitted, "Okay, so there's the first lesson. That makes a little more sense and I can see why you say we should find out what our talents and abilities are. But . . ." I paused. My answer made me think of a different question.

"How are people supposed to find out what their talents are, if they don't already know?"

"That is a good question—how does somebody find out? I'm not sure there's only one answer, but since we've been using Amanda as an example, let's look at her. How did she come to find out? She found out through experience. After taking a class she knew that's where she wanted to use her talent. Something inside clicked with her and told her that she would find happiness and fulfillment in doing stained glass. I would say that's probably one of the primary ways people can find out—through the everyday experiences they have that lead them to an understanding of their special gifts.

"Or, there is an additional way you might look at it. If Amanda didn't have to worry about making any money and she had the time, would she still want to do stained glass?"

"Absolutely, I have no doubt in my mind."

"Well there's another place a person could start. You could look at what you do now and ask yourself if you didn't have to work for money and had all the time you wanted, would you still do it? If the answer is no, then try and think about what you would do, given the same scenario. As you said earlier, Amanda doesn't even see it as work."

I had to summarize before he went any further. "Okay, so there's different ways to find out what your seeds are. The important thing is that you try to find out. Once you do find out, then you will be able to get past just being content, and as you say, find more fulfillment."

"That's right, except you left a part out. It's not the finding out that makes a person happy; you actually have to apply it in your life. Knowing what your gifts are does nobody any good if you don't use them," he said, pointing out my error.

"But if somebody has an idea of what their talents and abilities are, why wouldn't they want to use them, especially if they know they would really enjoy it?"

"Well," Lewis answered, "it could be a number of reasons: not enough time, not enough money, or they think it's unrealistic. They make future decisions based on present circumstances, seeing only where they are, instead of where they could be.

"And to be truthful, a lot of times it's hard to use our talents and abilities. When we come to recognize what they are and have never used them before, it can be way outside of our comfort zone."

Lewis slowly leaned forward and drew me in for his next statement. "The key to remember, Chris, and part of the second lesson, comes down to understanding one important truth: we are given our talents and abilities so that we can grow and learn; but more importantly, we are given them to share with others. We have them to serve the people around us so that we can help each other grow."

As his words sank into my mind, he pulled out of his shirt pocket the apple seed. He held it in front of him, looked past the seed, directly at me, and asked, "It's possible to find out how many seeds are in an apple, but is it possible to find out how many apples are in a seed?"

I looked at the seed and quietly responded, "No, it would be almost impossible."

"You could never really know, could you?" Lewis added. "One seed, if planted, could produce a whole apple tree, which in turn would produce apples every year." As he talked, he continued to turn the seed around in between his fingers. "Then the apples that they produce also have seeds in them. How many more trees would come from those seeds?"

I couldn't count that high, but Lewis had proved his point—there was potential for an infinite number of apples.

"That is why we need to realize what our gifts are, so that we can share them with others. If we serve others with our unique gifts, and then they hopefully serve others by sharing their unique gifts, then everybody benefits. It would be virtually impossible to count the good that comes from it."

I nodded, my mouth half open, as he resituated himself in his chair, becoming more excited with each phrase he uttered.

"Say there is something I've always wanted to do, but for whatever reason, including the ones we mentioned, I never do. I may feel a little guilty at first, or get down on myself, because I wasn't able to accomplish it. But over time, the guilt leaves, and I continue on my way, till one day I even forget what it was that I wanted to do.

"The problem is, we don't even realize that when we hold ourselves back, we are actually cheating others out of the good we could have done for them."

It was so much information to take in all at once. I got out of my chair and started to slowly pace.

"Amanda would work for free because she doesn't work to get paid; she works to share her talent, to serve. The money just happens to be a nice benefit, but it's not what brings her the happiness."

"So are you saying that people shouldn't worry about money?" I asked.

"Not at all. People have to make a living and provide for their family; that is just a fact of life. But why not do something you enjoy? If it means you need to have a less extravagant lifestyle because less money is coming in, isn't it worth it in order to truly love what you do? Or to look at it from another perspective, your talents and abilities may lead you to serve people in a way that does bring you wealth and prosperity.

"I've seen heads of corporations who make enough money to feed a small nation who are genuinely happy. I've also met some who make you wonder how they find any positive reason to get out of bed in the morning. There are teachers on this campus that may not make a lot of money, but they look forward to coming into work everyday of the year. Then there are others whose negative attitude rubs off on everyone around them.

"Talents and abilities come in all different shapes and sizes: construction workers, Olympians, ministers, senators, policemen, homemakers, entrepreneurs, and even volunteers. You can't just look at somebody and what they may be doing with their life, and decide whether they're happy or not. We can't point any fingers; we can only be true to ourselves in deciding what it is we really want to do. Not because it may pay more than something else, but because we want to do it more than anything else. Once we find it, we need to be willing to sacrifice our fears and worries so that we can try and make a difference."

After pacing back and forth, I walked over to the window. I rested my arm on the pane, thinking, while watching Lewis's reflection off the glass. The fountain below stayed steady and calm.

"To put it simply, I believe that we can only find true happiness when, without thought of our own reward, we get outside of ourselves and share our talents and abilities with those around us. Nobody can do everything, so we all have to do something."

As he paused, I continued to stare at the fountain, waiting for the water to burst. Lewis let out a sigh, as if to regroup after his winded speech.

"Sorry if I got a little excited. I know it's probably a lot to take in."

"No, no, it's fine," I said hesitantly. "You don't have to apologize; I'm just trying to get it all straight in my mind. You just . . . you just offer a different way at looking at things, that's all."

"Well I hope it doesn't shake your faith, too much," he said sarcastically, as he got up and walked over next to me at the window. "So what do you think?"

After taking a deep breath, I continued to look out over the fountain. "Well, on the surface, it kind of sounds too good to be true. But . . . but the more I think about it, it's hard not to agree with."

Feeling confused and a little uncomfortable by the seriousness of the whole discussion, I tried to lighten the tone a little. "Yep, you just make too much sense, old man."

Lewis laughed. "Yes, I am old, and although I've seen plenty of things that don't make sense, I've seen plenty of things that do." His voice became hushed. "The key is not to forget the ones that do."

We both stood in silence, looking out the window. I crossed my arms, trying to decide a final verdict on what Lewis had been sharing. To try and do so, at least then, was fruitless. Besides, he still owed me one more lesson. But that could wait for another time; as it stood, I already had too much to think about.

I thanked him for his thoughts; making sure my tone had more sincerity than the 'thank you's' in the past.

"One more thing you may want to think about," Lewis blurted out before I made my way down the steps. The last thing I needed was one more thing to think about; but I stopped to listen.

"I said at the beginning that I hope this helps you in your life in trying to figure everything out. Forgetting about what roads other people have chosen, you might stop to ask yourself if you could do anything, what would you do?"

My eyes were glued on the floor; I did not know what to say. The past few months of complaining and whining about school and work replayed in my mind.

"Thanks, Lewis." My feet seemed to drag down the steps. I felt as if a heavy cloth had been placed over me.

If you could do anything . . .

Honestly, I didn't know what I would do.
But I knew it wasn't social work.

10

Hopelessness

By the time I reached my apartment door all I wanted to do was get inside and relax. Mentally and physically I was drained. The things Lewis had shared with me had been running through my head non-stop. In my heart I wanted to believe it. The way he made it sound, it wasn't hard; just figure out your seeds and go for it. But my mind kept pulling me back into reality.

I knew there were probably other things I would enjoy more than social work, but I was already in the master's program, we had a kid on the way—there wasn't time to be anything but realistic. If your seeds called for a major life change, you couldn't just pick up and do it overnight, right?

Either way, I was sick of worrying about it.

I was hoping my mind would get some rest that night, because my body wouldn't. Amanda informed me that she wanted to start working on the nursery. We hadn't talked about what it was going to look like, but knowing her, it was going to be something extravagant. It wouldn't matter if I liked it or not; I would just be there for grunt work. Every now and then it would have been nice to get my two-cents in, but if I had learned one thing during the previous eight months, it was that one should not argue with a pregnant woman.

As the baby kept getting bigger, Amanda kept getting cuter. Of course, she didn't think so, but she was dealing with hormone surges and weird food cravings, so she wasn't entitled to an opinion.

Only three more weeks—I couldn't believe it.

"Amanda, I'm home," I bellowed in my not so perfect Ricky Ricardo voice. There was no response.

The note on the fridge said she had to run to the store to pick up some stuff. On the counter was an opened envelope with a card next to it . . .

Hope all's well. Go get something nice for yourself!
Love, Mom

My mother had to be the only woman in the world who would mail a gift certificate to someone she saw on a weekly basis. I was looking forward to Amanda being home, but if the stuff she was getting was free, well, I could entertain myself for a while.

I poured a drink, sat down in the glider rocker, and just let my whole body slowly switch to vegetable mode. As I swiveled around in the chair, I couldn't help but notice that our apartment was not very big. Especially with our first child coming soon, the apartment would all of a sudden become immensely smaller.

We only had two bedrooms, and one of those was going to be the baby's room. Where would the bookshelf, computer desk, and other stuff fit? What about highchairs, playpens, and poopy diaper pails? It was gradually sinking in more and more each day that we were really going to have a baby, and things were going to change—big time.

After school was done, I would get a job somewhere in Richmond. Starting off, my hours would probably be sporadic, mostly in the afternoon and evening, eventually leading more into the day as I got some experience behind me. Then we'd start looking for a house and have to pay a mortgage, property taxes, and homeowners insurance—all the signs of true adulthood.

I would be able to play with the baby in the morning a little bit before work, and then hopefully for a few minutes in the evening. Eventually, the baby would not be a baby anymore, and would require all the activities of a child: school, piano lessons, and sports. I considered soccer a good sport, especially for little kids. At that age, it was a mass of three-feet-tall little people moving in a big cluster up and down the field.

Our first child would start school, and by then our second would be born. School plays and parent teacher conferences would be regular stops, if my schedule allowed me to go.

Over time, there would be a salary cap at whatever agency I was working. To make myself more marketable, I would probably need to go and get my doctorate. That would bring in more income and allow me more opportunities. It would also get me back in the classroom for another two years, and then I'd spend another two on my dissertation.

The second child would be walking and we'd have our hands full, especially Amanda. There would have to be time scheduled each week just so we could see each other. But with work and school, she'd be supportive and understanding; knowing that I was just trying to provide for the family.

By the time I finished my dissertation, there would be three little rug rats running around, which would probably call for an end to any procreative powers we had left. A few more years of clinical work and I would probably get hired on as a faculty member at a local university. A career as a professional educator didn't sound all that bad. It seemed that being a professor, even though low on the totem pole, would be a desired change of atmosphere.

There would probably be some rocky spots along the way, but we would manage. Besides, there were plenty of other people worse off than us, right?

While I had been planning out the future, my drink had run out, my stomach was screaming for food, and I realized that the apartment was freezing. I turned on the heater and walked to the fridge to get a look at the dinner options.

"Everything is going to change," I reminded myself one more time.

I awoke to the heavy sound of a fist on the front door, and two bites of my dinner left on the paper plate in my lap. My neck was sore from being bent backward, and my hand was asleep. After straightening my glasses I barely made out the VCR clock—10:50 p.m. Amanda sure had been out late. I figured her haul was so big she didn't have a free hand to open the door.

"Did you buy the whole . . .?" I started to ask as I opened the door, to find a uniformed police officer standing before me. I didn't know what he was doing there, but I had seen too many movies to think it was something positive. My eyes glanced past him to see if there was anyone else with him. He was alone.

"May I help you, officer?"

"Mr. Chris Sorensen?"

"Yes, what's the matter?" My blood pressure raced and my hands became moist. He looked almost as nervous as I felt.

Before he got a word out, I could read it in his face. "Where is she?"

"She's at Richmond Regional. We tried to call but never got through." Amanda usually turned the ringer off in the evening to avoid telemarketing calls.

After I realized that my keys were still in my pocket, I left the police officer standing at my open door while I pushed the elevator button to go down.

When the elevator door opened, the officer softly said, "She did not make it, Mr. Sorensen."

My lips trembled as the door started to close. Before it shut completely, I could still see a portion of him through the shaft as he finished his statement.

"But your son did."

11

Wandering

October seventeenth. The day my son was born. The day my wife died.

I wanted to hide. I did not want to talk to anybody or do anything. I just wanted to be upset and angry; it seemed easier than trying to figure out why.

But I couldn't.

I held my newborn son in my arms as his mother was laid to rest on a clear, cold afternoon. I didn't have time to ask why. I had given all I could to my wife, and now I had to give all I could to Michael.

Even though I knew what I had to do, closure didn't come. I just couldn't let it.

It didn't seem right to let everything go and say it was over, and then move on. I knew that was what I needed to do, and I knew I could do it, but saying goodbye, laying everything to rest, laying Amanda to rest . . .

I was doing it physically, but I didn't know if I would ever be able to do it mentally.

While my son quietly slept in my arms, the casket slowly found its way into the grave. When the time came, how was I going to tell him?

The memory of Amanda lying peacefully on the hospital bed, with covers and blankets over her, is not how I wanted to see her for the last time. But it was better than being on the scene. Just thinking about what it might have looked like . . .

I just tried to block it out.

Michael was three weeks premature, which usually would not have been a major concern, but there were some precautions the doctors wanted to take because of the crash. I didn't leave his side the entire time he was in the hospital. It was my way to show him, and Amanda, that I was sorry for not being there. Sorry it wasn't me, instead of her. Sorry it had to be either of us—if it had to be either of us at all.

One of the hardest things I found in trying to deal with everything was that there was no one to blame: the other driver, Amanda, or even myself. It was nobody's fault, it just happened. It would have been so much easier to handle if somebody could have been blamed. So I got mad at the only one left—God.

Mad at Him for taking my wife, mad at Him for leaving me alone to raise Michael, and mad at Him for having all the control.

But even that only lasted for so long.

After a few days of depression and self-pity, my dad offered some humble, sincere advice. He wasn't preachy, and he didn't lecture me; he just passed on something from his heart. "I can't imagine what you're going through, son, but I would think that being angry with the one you hope is taking care of Amanda now is . . . well, it would be, for lack of a better word, son, wrong."

My dad never really had a way with words, but most times he was on target with the things he did say.

Deep down I wasn't a very religious person, by some standards anyway, but I fully believed she was safe in His care. I was the one, for whatever reason, left to take care of Michael. I didn't have time to be angry, or upset, or selfish; but sometimes I still wanted to hide. Luckily, I had family that would not let me. I was thankful I didn't even have a chance to try.

I didn't know what I would do if my parents were not willing to look after Michael. Lord knows I did not want to leave him with a baby sitter or in a day care. I just didn't want to leave him, period. I never imagined I would move back home, especially at twenty-five years old. I never imagined I'd be a widower at twenty-five, either.

Even though I was staying together, it still seemed like there was always going to be something missing. Like life was going to be nonstop, twenty-four hours a day, seven days a week, forever. Wanting to be with Michael and finishing school and getting a job and . . .

I just wanted it all to come together.

I tried to hold all the hurt in for Michael. At least that's what I told myself. I thought holding it in would help me stay strong. But the night before the funeral, as I brought him home from the hospital, I cried.

To be honest, most nights I cried.

Michael let out a whimper, and as I finally remembered where I was, the preacher finished the service, "Ashes to ashes, dust to dust. Amen."

Everyone slowly backed away from the grave. My mother touched my shoulder and gave Michael a glance. She was always a very perceptive woman.

Handing him to her, I kissed her on the cheek, and slowly made my way to the grave. Silent and alone, kneeling, nothing came to mind. As the seconds passed I did not say anything, and Amanda did not say anything back. There, together, quiet, the thought of our wedding day raced into my mind and a flood of emotions hit me in an instant. She was the best thing that had ever happened to me. I didn't know how I was going to stay sane without her.

I tried to say something. I tried to say anything. I even tried to cry. But nothing would come—no words, no tears.

The greatest thing in my life, the closest friend in my life . . . my whole life had been taken away.

I couldn't believe it was happening.

❖   ❖   ❖

I only had a month and a half left in the semester. The university was very understanding about my situation, and by the time I finally brought Michael home, they granted me an additional week off without revoking any of my earned credit. All the material and text that I needed to digest had been taken care of already. The only things left to do were final exams and an unfinished project. It was going to mean an extremely busy New Year, but it was better then getting an incomplete grade and having to make up all of the work.

Work had been equally generous, allowing me to take some time off. For a while, there appeared to be at least a gleam of hope that something would go right. At that time in my life, things needed to go right.

With the newfound responsibility of being a single parent, I felt that my attitude about school, work, and my major in general would change. I would mentally be able to block out the problems and look for the good. I was supposed to grin and bear it, right? That's what being unselfish and sacrificing for the family was all about, wasn't it? Unfortunately, the feelings only got worse. Once my excused absence was up and I started back into the daily grind, it seemed that all my reasons for getting my degree in social work slowly faded away.

Regarding work and school, I went from dealing with them, to accepting them, to lack of interest, all the way up to despising them. Without Amanda, the only reason I felt compelled to stick it out in the first place was gone, too.

All of my talks with Lewis played over in my mind. I knew I had only been fooling myself. Just two days, two lousy days back into the routine, and just the thought of finishing school, not to mention choosing it as a career, depressed me.

My parents had been extremely patient and helpful, but I couldn't talk to them about it. They would give me the "I have a responsibility now" speech: I had to sacrifice my interests for Michael and think about what was best for him.

I couldn't talk to any of my fellow workers or classmates, mostly because I didn't know them that well. And I couldn't talk to Amanda. The problem was, I should have talked to her to begin with. It made it hard, looking back and knowing that she would have supported me.

I only had one unbiased opinion left to turn to.

I couldn't believe it had been two weeks since I'd seen him. He probably didn't have a clue what was going on. And to think, after all that time, he never even met Amanda. We just put it off one day too many.

"Chris, I'm sorry about Amanda," Lewis said as I made my way into the mezzanine. He had a look of sincerity, a look of empathy I would never forget.

"I hope you haven't been waiting for me too long?"

"No, no. I just got up here a little while ago. I knew, or was hoping, you would turn up here again sooner or later."

How did he know? I had been trying to figure out how I was going to tell him, and he already knew. He must have read it in the obituary, or seen it on the news, or something. It was a big story around Richmond, especially because Michael lived. "Nothing short of a miracle," everyone said.

"She was the best thing that ever happened to me."

"She *is* the best thing that ever happened to you," Lewis said.

Nodding, I exhaled.

We spent the next few hours just talking and sharing feelings. I talked about Amanda, Michael, and my new responsibility. It was bittersweet. I wouldn't trade my son for anything. He was like a small extension of me, both body and soul. I loved him with all of my heart. But it took losing my wife to have him with me. Why did there have to be a compromise?

During our talk, Lewis, with his curly white hair, his rough hands, and his gargantuan smile, made me feel like the most important person on earth. I relished in it for as long as possible, until it was time for me to go to work.

"I'll see you on Tuesday, Lewis"

"You just hang in there, Chris," he said with a wink. Then he thought for a moment and hesitantly added, "And if you find yourself this weekend, just thinking about whatever, ponder on the things we've talked about."

I could tell he wanted to say more, but he didn't want to say too much, which at the time, I appreciated.

"I will, Lewis."

When I reached the doorway I turned back toward him. "And thank you for being here for me."

"Anytime Chris, anytime." Smiling warmly he added, "That's what I'm here for."

12

Coming to *Terms*

I couldn't do anything else.

I just sat there and stared at him; stared at him while he was sleeping.

Sometimes at night I'd dream about being in the delivery room with Amanda—pushing, breathing, maybe a few targeted remarks at me about being responsible for "this," or just plain anger at me for being male. Hearing that first cry from my son, cutting the cord, holding him and my beautiful wife, and taking that first picture—that is how I saw it, just like we had planned it. Then Michael would start to cry, and I would wake up.

But that night was different.

He was sleeping, peacefully, right next to me in the bed. Emotionally, he was just taking Amanda's place. I couldn't help but stare at him: his dark hair, his big blue eyes, his small fingers and skinny legs. He was perfect.

I turned to lie on my back and gazed out the window. A faint hint of light coming from the neighbor's house danced off the trees as the wind blew. While staring through the pane, Lewis's comment came to mind.

Just ponder on the things we've talked about.

What about my talents and abilities? What about my seeds? What about my gifts? What about Michael? What would he grow up to be? What would he grow up to do? What did I want to teach him? What would I be able to teach him? Would it make a difference?

Would he be happy?

Would I be happy?

Sadly enough, I knew the answer to the question. Yes. I would be happy with everything— except doing social work. I enjoyed working with people and I knew I could do some good, but if I were to keep going forward with it, it wouldn't . . . it wouldn't be right.

There was something pulling me toward a different path, a different way. A feeling that social work was not the right direction for my abilities, for my talents, for my gifts. For some, social work was their seed. For others it might mean being a doctor, a plumber, or a construction worker. For others it might come through being a teacher, a Cub Scout leader, a baseball player, a musician, or a secretary. Money didn't matter, fame didn't matter—it was all about service.

Deep down in my heart I knew, or at least had an idea, of what I could do, what I wanted to do. But I was too afraid of failing. I was too busy staying busy to take some time and some faith to realize I could be of more service going down a different road, making different choices, one where I would be happy.

talents . . . abilities . . . service . . . happiness . . .

I sat straight up in bed and turned on the lamp. My eyes widened and my thoughts started to take off in a thousand different directions.

But I did not let them.

I already knew the answer, and I wasn't going to let myself think my way out of it. I wasn't going to leave it to chance.

A feeling of surety and peace went rushing through me. The only way I could express how I felt was by smiling from ear to ear. I looked at Michael and whispered.

"Well, buddy, he is right after all!"

I could not lie to myself anymore.

13

Direction and a *Proposal*

School was a joy and everything seemed to be falling into place and I knew why, which made it even better.

Of course, when I changed majors everyone thought I was crazy. My parents and the rest of my family wondered why I switched being almost halfway into the program. In a way, it was a little crazy, I guess. But that's okay. Being true to myself, it actually felt as if a burden had been lifted off my shoulders. The price I would have to pay seemed more than reasonable.

I took Lewis's advice and thought about what I would do if I didn't have to worry about money; what I would do if I could do it for free. And the answer came. Simply, surely, it came that I would want to work with youth.

I remember thinking that it would be a good experience for me to work with the youth at the agency, but I never got the opportunity. Or, I should say, I never took the opportunity. The more I thought about it, the more I realized that I did not want to focus on helping youth overcome problems; I wanted to focus on helping them avoid problems.

So that was where I found myself. I switched my degree, and was going to get my master's in education, with an emphasis in counseling—I wanted to be a high school guidance counselor. I know it may sound silly, but even saying it got me excited. Just that one little switch, that one little change, made a world of difference.

I thought it was going to have to be a huge switch, something dramatic. The way Lewis made it sound it was a pretty big step. But over time I realized that a big step did not have to be measured by distance—it could be measured by direction.

A few of my classes, two to be exact, switched over to the education program, which did not have an advanced degree. Two classes wasn't a lot, but it was enough to make it possible for me to finish the degree in a year and a half. It was hard to imagine that Michael would be 18 months old when I graduated. He would be walking, talking some, and able to give me high five. He was my pride and joy.

Thinking about my circumstances, I couldn't help but feel that there was someone's hand in all of it: someone helping me out with Michael, with school, and with my book.

That's right, I decided I was going to write a book. I couldn't believe it myself. Me, a writer? I never even considered myself a reader; much less someone to actually put a story together, but Lewis's books put a bug in me that I couldn't seem to get rid of.

Every few days I would sneak some out of the mezzanine, and they really opened my eyes. They all had different stories to share, but in some way, each of them helped me learn new things and see life in a different perspective.

So I decided that if there were other people out there who had a story to tell, why not me? Why not? Anything was possible, right? At least Lewis encouraged me to go for it, which at the time was enough encouragement for me.

I didn't see him as much after changing my major. We only were able to get together on Saturdays because of my new class schedule, and living with my parents made it a longer drive to and from school. Because we met on Saturdays, and I didn't have classes, I was able to bring Michael along.

He really enjoyed the trips to the library and had grown quite fond of Lewis. I think Lewis enjoyed the visits more than Michael did, even though he wouldn't admit it.

That old man had taught me a lot. One of the biggest reasons his words stuck with me so powerfully was because he never pressured me. He never tried to force any of his ideas on me, even though he was very adamant about them.

I think that was one of his seeds.

But there was still one more. There was still the third lesson that Lewis had not shared with me yet. It's not that I had forgotten about it, I just hadn't asked him for it. Up till then, I didn't feel ready. But I decided it was time. My life was finally in focus.

❖   ❖   ❖

"What move should I make, Mikey?" Lewis asked, and then waited for a response. After a few gurgles and a smile, Lewis nodded his head. "I think you're right." It was amazing how they actually seemed to communicate with each other.

"Well, Lewis," I blurted suddenly, not able to hold it in anymore, "I think I'm ready."

He made his move without looking at me. "Ready for what?"

"I'm ready for the final thing, the third lesson. I've been thinking about it, and I finally feel like I have a grasp on the first two and I'm ready for the third."

"Are you sure you're ready for it?" he asked, finally looking at me.

"Yes, I'm sure."

He nodded, with his lips pursed, and then asked, "Just for fun, how about a little proposal?"

"What is it?" As long as he didn't make me beg, I would do anything.

"I have a suspicion you are better at chess than you put on. I think you really do know what you're doing, you just don't really care." He paused, leaned back in his chair, and continued. "And to be honest, after a gazillion games I'm getting bored winning all the time. I will give you my final thought, but you have to beat me first."

I sighed inside—maybe I would never find out. But a little competitive proposal was exactly what I needed. "You're on, Lewis. I'm even feeling lucky today."

I reached out and moved my son's stroller closer to me. "And you're not getting any help from Michael, either."

"Well, then there's another stipulation as well."

"What? You can't have two."

"I most certainly can," he said smugly. "I have something you want, and you have something I want."

"What are you talking about?"

"Your manuscript. First you have to beat me at chess, and then you have to let me read your manuscript when it is finished. As soon as you can do those two things, you can have it." With a victory

tory grin covering his face, he began studying his fingernails.

If he hadn't been so close to dying, I would have killed him myself.

"You're on," I responded boldly.

Unfortunately, that didn't turn out to be the day that I accomplished the first part of the deal. Sadly enough, he beat me even faster than normal. But I knew it would come. It would just take time.

I only hoped it wouldn't take too much.

14

Checkmate

I hadn't really thought about how things would fall into place after I graduated and the book was done. What if I couldn't get a job anywhere? What if nothing ever happened with the book? The list went on and on.

But I couldn't keep sitting there just wondering what if—I had to stay focused and take it one day at a time. One step in front of the other, that's how I had to move along. With my attention span, it was hard, but it was the only way I knew of to get where I wanted to be.

It was actually a blessing that Lewis used the manuscript as a challenge. I knew I would eventually get it done, but since I had never written a book before, it probably would have taken forever. Unfortunately, I didn't have forever. There was no way I would let Lewis leave this world after giving me only two of his three lessons.

In order to keep myself on pace, I got up at six every morning to make sure I had at least two hours to work on the book. Michael usually slept well from 5a.m. till about 9 or 10a.m., so that was my only chance to write in peace. As hard as writing was, it didn't compare to the frustration I felt each time Lewis put me in checkmate. Finishing the manuscript was completely under my control, but conquering Lewis, that was a little more involved.

❖   ❖   ❖

I finally did it. Nine weeks after extending the challenge, I put Lewis into checkmate. I knew it would only be a matter of time. I think it was more the law of numbers working in my favor than actual skill, but I would take luck over skill any day.

What a blessed day it was!

He must not have believed that I could actually beat him. He took it pretty hard.

"One down Lewis and only one more to go."

Trying to figure out where he had gone wrong, he just stared at the board.

"It's pointless, old man. You lost, fair and square. And just to warn you, I am almost done with my manuscript. You should have it this time next week," I said, matter-of-factly, still not knowing for sure if I could finish it that quickly. I was close to being done, but there were still some areas to smooth out.

But I needed to get something to him, even if it was not the actual final draft. I just wouldn't bother to tell him it was still in the works. Finals were the following week, which meant I had to spend most of my time studying. He would be lucky to get anything.

"I thought you said writing was harder than you thought it would be?"

"At first it was, but the more I write, the easier it gets to transfer the words from my brain to paper. I'm almost done, although I'm still having trouble thinking of a title. Either way, you better be prepared. Next Saturday you owe me."

As I walked out the door, I quickly looked over my shoulder to see Lewis still staring at the board. It was kind of sad to see someone who couldn't take defeat.

But only kind of—he was getting no pity from me.

15

A Discovery

The copy center on campus took forever with the manuscript. I made a fancy little cover for it and everything. The only thing missing was a title. I wasn't ready to publish it yet, it still had to be professionally edited, but just to have the foundation done felt great.

It even felt better than beating Lewis at chess.

I didn't take Michael with me because I had no idea how long it would take at the copiers. It turned out to be the smart move. I only needed one copy, and it still took almost half an hour. Michael would have driven me, and everyone else in line, crazy.

I finally arrived at the library and made my way through the atrium, up the stairs to the second floor, straight to the computer tables, right at the card file, down the hallway, up the staircase and into my sanctuary—which was completely empty.

There was nothing: no tables, no chairs, no bookshelves, no books, and no Lewis.

It didn't make any sense.

I tried to recall if Lewis had mentioned anything about having the room cleaned, but nothing came to mind. That was the only rational conclusion I could come up with as to why everything was gone.

Confusion hung over me as I made my way back down the steps. I just wanted to find Lewis; he would hopefully know what was going on. Walking back towards the entrance, I stopped at the information desk.

"I'm looking for someone and was wondering if you could page him for me," I asked the receptionist.

"Sure," she said politely, "what's the name?" She picked up the microphone and looked at me, waiting for me to answer.

I paused, and then said with reluctance, "Lewis." I didn't know his last name. I had never asked and he had never said.

"Uh . . . just page Lewis."

She lowered the microphone from her mouth, looking at me for a little more information. The only other thing I could think to say was, "Lewis, the volunteer."

Out of sheer politeness, she paged, "Lewis the volunteer."

After paging him, she asked me to take a seat on one of the chairs next to the desk. My eyes started wandering as I waited impatiently.

I noticed the windows above the foyer that looked down from what had become my second home. I couldn't believe that it had been well over a year since I first stepped foot up there.

I started thinking about all that had taken place, and suddenly remembered the manuscript in my hand. In my recollecting, I was wringing it in between my palms. I quickly stopped, not wanting to give Lewis a wrinkled copy.

My knees were crossed and my foot shook furiously. A few minutes had already passed.

I stood and walked over to the receptionist. "If you don't mind, could you please page him again? I would really appreciate it."

She repeated the page.

While walking back to the chair, I noticed an entranceway to a small waiting room. I had seen it before, but I always headed up to the second floor as fast as possible. I walked past the chair I had been sitting in and took a right into the tiny foyer.

There was a large oak table in the center of the room surrounded by dark brown couches. Small lights mounted on the ceiling gave the room just enough light to see the large, life sized paintings of the former library presidents hanging on the wall. Quietly, I strolled around and read the biographical plaques that accompanied each painting.

Then I saw it. A picture of Lewis?

I laughed to myself. Lewis—a former president of the library?

The closer, longer I stared, the stranger it got. The plaque next to the painting did not say that Lewis was, or used to be, a president; it said that Lewis was a beneficiary. But not just a beneficiary; he was the beneficiary. He was the lone monetary source for the remodeling of the L. J. Anderson library—the Lewis James Anderson library.

Gazing, my mouth still open, I finished reading the plaque—and my spine tingled.

Lewis James Anderson
Beneficiary
1927-1999

16

The Exchange

After I saw the picture in the library, I had to
feel for the chair behind me to sit down. I rotated
between looking at the picture, my feet, and then
the picture again. I did not feel anything: no sad-
ness, no despair. I didn't know what to feel, what
to think. But something must have shown in my
expression.

"Are you all right?" The man standing behind
me was one of the vice presidents of the library. He
had been watching me through his office window.

"I'm fine," I replied.

He was about to walk away when out of a need
to know more, to know something, I asked, pointing
to Lewis's picture, "Did you know this man?"

"I sure did," he said, walking closer to the picture and giving it a respectful glance. "One of the greatest men I have ever known."

I asked him some questions about Lewis, and he had nothing but praise for him. Lewis was a good man, very wealthy, who loved to read, and just wanted to help. Lewis gave a little over four million dollars to help pay for the remodeling of the library. But Lewis specifically said the mezzanine could not be touched because he wanted to have somewhere quiet where he could take a break during his volunteer hours. Mr. Nielson said Lewis wanted to stick around and make sure everything stayed in order. He didn't mention how Lewis had made his money, which I was curious in finding out about, but I didn't say anything. It was hard to say anything—it seemed so unreal.

Mr. Nielson also mentioned attending the funeral. "Let's see, it's now September, so . . ." he thought to himself for a second. "If I remember correctly, it will be two years ago this coming May." Two years in May meant that Lewis had passed away the month before Amanda and I moved back to Richmond.

I wanted to faint. I glared past Mr. Nielson and heard him without seeing him. It was as if time stood still.

He said Lewis was buried in the old Southside Cemetery. He couldn't remember exactly where, but he knew it was near the pond. After pausing for a second, giving me a steady glance, eyebrow raised, he asked, "Why do you want to know about him?" I blinked and regained my senses. I needed to get out of there.

"Oh, I already knew a little about him. I just had a few missing pieces." I thanked him for his time and left him standing there. Practically running to my car, I couldn't think about anything but getting to the cemetery.

I had been to the cemetery before, but only once.

The father of a childhood friend passed away when we were in the eighth grade, and he asked me to go and help him be strong. He was pretty scared. I was too. I still remember driving past the pond toward the little canopy where the grave had been dug. I wasn't sure what to think about death. It seemed so distant.

"Maybe I am dreaming," I said to myself as I reached the gated entrance to the cemetery. I stopped before I entered. I still didn't know what to think about it. Even after Amanda died, it was all so vague and unsure.

She was buried in a different cemetery on the other side of town. The only solace I could find after her death was going to visit her every Sunday with Michael. Most of the time I didn't say anything, I would just sit and play with my son, and talk to the wind—talk to Amanda. It was difficult at first, but it was the only way I could think of to keep her with me. It was the only way I could think of to keep her with Michael.

I drove passed the large, metal gate, toward the pond, and parked near the north shore. There were no parking spaces; just a dirt clearing. Over the years the pond had become a place where parents brought their children to feed the ducks. The cars had worn down the grass next to the pond so much that they finally decided to go ahead and clear it away and use it as permanent parking.

After I parked the car, I noticed a mother next to the pond with her son tossing pieces of bread in the water.

Maybe death wasn't as distant as I thought.

Not knowing where to start, I tried to calmly stroll around the pond, while glancing at the various markers. But I was anything but calm. I did not want to see the grave, if it was really there at all.

Some raindrops splashed through the top of the pond as the wind started to blow. I folded my arms to try and block out the light, chilly breeze. The weatherman had called for rain that morning; I should have listened.

The rain came down just hard enough to cause the few people next to the pond to hurry off to their cars and call it a day. I continued my search while the sun peeked in and out of the clouds.

I couldn't believe how many different grave markers there were: big ones, little ones, stone, marble, crosses and everything in-between. If the choice had been left up to Lewis, I knew his gravestone would be simple but powerful, not obtrusive or ostentatious. But it might not have been up to him, especially if he was as admired and wealthy as Mr. Nielson said he was.

I didn't know what to think; it was like some kind of bad dream. I was trying to find the grave of my best friend—who had been dead ever since I met him.

But as soon as I saw the marker, the dream ended.

It was on the south side of the pond; not far from the shore. The marker was marble, medium in size, nothing out of the ordinary, kind of rounded at the top, and polished to a shine. The flowers arranged in front swayed lightly as I read the inscription:

Lewis James Anderson
Beloved Husband, Father, and Citizen
He Touched More Lives Than He Will Ever Know

I expected to feel some type of sorrow or pain, but it only felt like reality was finally setting in. It was as if some part of me, deep down inside, thought Lewis was too good to be true from the start.

The wind and rain died down and the sun started to come out slightly from behind the clouds. I bent down on one knee and rubbed my finger over his name.

"How come you never told me?"

I almost grinned. I knew the answer, but it would have been nice to hear it from him. Whatever he had to transcend in order to be with me, I was thankful for it. It didn't have to make sense. Like Amanda being gone, it might not ever make sense.

Maybe some things just don't have to.

"Excuse me."

I stood up, startled. I gave my attention to a woman standing behind me. The wind started to blow lightly again.

"Did you know this man?" she asked. A pleasant looking black lady stood before me, probably in her late 40's or early 50's, medium height, fit, with a pair of the clearest eyes I had ever seen. The only thing out of place was the curly white hair on the head of someone who did not look old enough to deserve it. I thought of Lewis.

"Yes, I did," I answered and looked back down at the marker. "He was a good man."

"Yes," she replied, nodding as she looked at the grave marker, "he *is* a good man." I heard her take a deep breath, and then, slowly exhaling, she added, "I sure have missed him."

My heart stopped. As I glanced into her smiling face, something inside told me who she was. I stood perfectly still, gazing in utter amazement.

She didn't wait for me to respond. "I believe you have something for him," she said calmly, confidently, her hands crossing each other in front. It was probably easy for her to read my uncertainty. She smiled wider, as if to laugh to herself, and then she pointed down to my left hand.

"I said, I believe you have something for Lewis."

I forgot I was still holding the manuscript. Not knowing what to do, I had brought it with me, and if all else failed I was going to leave it on the grave. At least that way I could say I had kept my word.

Slowly, I handed it to her. She took it, placed it under her arm without looking at it, and put her hands in the pockets of her long over coat.

"So you finally got it done, huh?"

"Uh . . . yeah. For the most part."

I tried to find some way to make sense of what was going on. Nothing came, so I said the first thing that came to mind. "Given the recent discoveries in my life though, the ending will need to be changed a little."

"I think Lewis will understand," she answered, half laughing.

By her stance, I expected her to say goodbye and walk away, but she didn't. She was still standing there, like she was waiting for me to make the next move.

"Is . . ." I paused, searching for the words. She kept her focus on me. "Does he have something for me?"

"It took you long enough," she said. "I actually have three things for you."

She moved forward and, taking me by surprise, kissed my cheek. I could not feel her lips, but there was a warmth there stronger than any physical touch.

"That's from Amanda," she said softly, and my body shivered.

Then, leaning toward the grave, she reached her hand out and placed something on the top of the marker. "That's from Lewis."

She turned back toward me and kissed my other cheek.

"And that's from me. Thank you so much for answering his prayer," she said, with a tear in her eye, as she turned to leave.

"Wait," I said suddenly. She stopped and turned around.

"I thought he said you left him a long time ago?"

"I did," she said calmly, "and it is so good to have him back." She turned, and then walked away.

As she left, everything came together. I wanted to give her a message to share with Amanda, but something deep down told me she would—or that she didn't have to.

Amanda was nearby; I just couldn't see her.

I turned back to the grave to see what she had delivered from Lewis. Sitting on top of the grave was a chess piece—the king. It was the king from Lewis's chess set at the library.

Why would he leave me the king?

I glanced over his marker one more time, shaking my head in disbelief. Well, maybe not disbelief. With all that had happened, it was hard to disbelieve anything.

I got in my car and slowly headed for the entrance. The clouds had almost completely parted and the sun was shining. As I pulled onto the main street, something Lewis's wife had said rang curiously in my ears. I did not know what she meant.

Thank you so much for answering his prayer.

17

The Greatest Discovery

As I made my way into the library, I hid my face from the receptionist as best I could. I had already caused her enough grief for one day.

I was hoping for something different this time when I reached the mezzanine; maybe that everything would be back together and I'd realize that it really was a dream.

But it was still as I had left it—completely empty.

I glanced down again at the chess piece in my hand and my nerves started to get edgy. As long as the chess set was there, with an empty hook for the king, and the third lesson I'd been waiting for, everything would be okay.

> *You have been given unique talents and abili-*
> *ties. You have an obligation to realize what they*
> *are.*
>
> *You have been given these gifts to serve those*
> *around you. Such service is what will bring you*
> *true happiness.*

And then, hopefully, whatever was waiting within the elevator walls would finally bring it all together.

After gently separating the two doors of the elevator, I crouched down and made my way inside. I reached and opened the compartment that housed the chess set.

It was still there. A sigh of relief escaped me. The clasps on the sides came undone and the wooden frame opened up to reveal the empty hook for the king. As I pulled the set completely open something fell to the floor, startling me.

I placed the set to the side and gently picked up the manila envelope that was lying in the small layer of dust next to my feet. My heart raced as I read the words written on the front of the envelope.

For Chris

I opened the envelope to find a stack of papers, about a half an inch thick, bound together by a black clasp. There was a hand written note that was paper clipped to the first page of the stack.

I know you've been patient, so I won't keep you wondering anymore. The third lesson, the greatest discovery Chris, is that . . .

. . . YOU HAVE A CHOICE.

Your seeds will not grow automatically. You have to want it, work for it, and decide each day that you will be closer than you were the day before. That is the difference between us as people and the rest of God's creations—he gave us the ability to choose for ourselves.

Sure, the first two lessons are important and make a difference, but if you don't choose to apply them, they do nobody any good. If you do decide to apply them Chris, I promise you, you will make a difference— even if sometimes you may not know how. And don't ever forget, even with all the good I know you plan to do, that the most important life you can touch is Michael's.

Well, that's the third thing I told you I would share with you. I encourage you to thank about it often. It's going to be tough sometimes, but it's getting through the tough times that brings the joy.

Now for a different matter. I want you to have the chess set—I don't think I could trust anybody else with it. Next, you'll find a key taped to the bottom of this note. Just follow the directions on the back of this page and they will lead you to the storage unit where I have my books packed away. I know you'll take good care of them, and don't just leave them sitting on the shelf; be sure to put them to use.

And lastly, this stack of papers is a small piece of my personal history. I know I never shared that much with you—hopefully you understand why—but this should make up for it. I never had a chance to tell it to all the people I wanted to, but you can be the one to answer my prayer, and see that it gets out to the world.

Well my friend, thank you for a wonderful journey, and be sure to enjoy the one that awaits you.

If you never stop believing in miracles, they will never stop coming true.

All the best,

Lewis

I took a deep breath to keep my composure, lifted the note, and read aloud the words on the first page, "Final Manuscript—written by Lewis J. Anderson."

He passed away before he had the chance to get it into print. That was how I could be the answer to his prayer.

Respectfully turning the pages, I glanced over the manuscript. I could hardly wait to see what events and experiences Lewis had to share with me as I read his words, his story . . .

The
Greatest
Choice

What is Lewis's story?

Be one of the first to find out
in the anticipated sequel to
The Greatest Discovery...

The

Greatest

Choice

Coming Soon

❖   ❖   ❖

Just visit:
<u>www.thegreatestdiscovery.com</u>
to join the e-mail list for updates.

———

POND
PUBLISHING
books to entertain & inspire

The author would love to hear from you.
If you have any thoughts or questions about the
book, you can contact him at:

Chris Sorensen
9947 Hull St. #197
Richmond, VA 23236

Or visit his website at:

www.thegreatestdiscovery.com

where you can e-mail Chris directly and join the e-
mail list to receive up-to-date information on new
titles and author events.

———————————————

Chris is available for speaking engagements.
If you would like to schedule him to speak to your
group—book club, school, church, business, etc.—
please visit the web site to see a list of topics Chris
presents on, or e-mail him a topic for consideration.
His e-mail address is:

chris@thegreatestdiscovery.com